Benjamin Franklin, Bliss Perry

Benjamin Franklin

Selections from Autobiography, Poor Richard's Almanac, Advice to a Young

Tradesman, The Whistle - Vol. 1

Benjamin Franklin, Bliss Perry

Benjamin Franklin
Selections from Autobiography, Poor Richard's Almanac, Advice to a Young Tradesman, The Whistle - Vol. 1

ISBN/EAN: 9783337118891

Printed in Europe, USA, Canada, Australia, Japan

Cover: Foto ©Raphael Reischuk / pixelio.de

More available books at **www.hansebooks.com**

Little Masterpieces

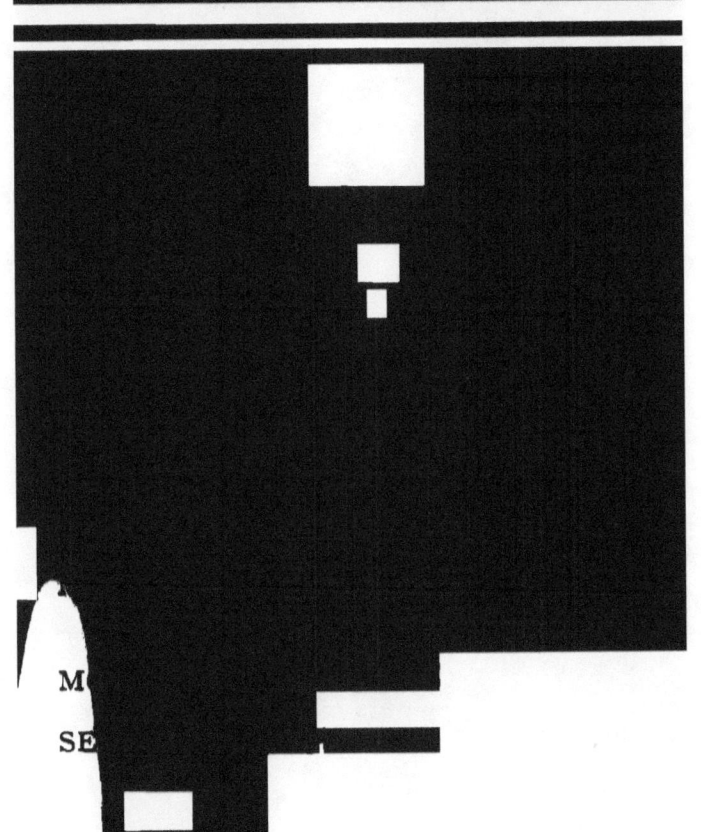

M

SE

Introduction

THIS volume of selections from the writings of Benjamin Franklin begins with a series of extracts from his "Autobiography." The occasion and motive for the composition of this work are explained in its opening paragraph. It was begun in 1771. Franklin, at that time residing in England as the agent of the American colonies, was enjoying a week's leisure at the country house of his friend Dr. Shipley, the Bishop of St. Asaph's. He was in his sixty-sixth year. The contrast between his present position of honor and influence and the narrow circumstances of his boyhood was striking, though the full force of Franklin's personality and his greatest services to his country were yet to be displayed.

It was for the perusal of his own family, apparently, that the memoirs were first undertaken, and there is no evidence that at this time Franklin considered the question of their ultimate publication. The composition was interrupted after he had told the story of his life up to the period of his marriage. Thirteen years later, in 1784, while living in France, he resumed his task. The blank line on page 78 of

Introduction

the present volume indicates the beginning of the second portion, and its conclusion will be found on page 102. The third and final section of the memoirs was written in Philadelphia in 1788, in the author's eighty-second year.

He writes under date of October 24th, 1788, to his friend Benjamin Vaughan, who had seen and praised the first part of his manuscript : " I am recovering from a long-continued gout, and am diligently employed in writing the History of my Life, to the doing of which the persuasions contained in your letter of January 31st, 1783, have not a little contributed. I am now in the year 1756, just before I was sent to England. To shorten the work, as well as for other reasons, I omit all facts and transactions that may not have a tendency to benefit the young reader, by showing him from my example, and my success in emerging from poverty, and acquiring some degree of wealth, power, and reputation, the advantages of certain modes of conduct which I observed, and of avoiding the errors which were prejudicial to me. If a writer can judge properly of his own work, I fancy, on reading over what is already done, that the book will be found entertaining, interesting, and useful, more so than I expected when I began it."

Entertaining, interesting, and useful the " Autobiography" surely is. The extracts chosen relate largely to Franklin's early life, and to the formation of his habits and charac-

Introduction

ter. His " Rules of Conduct," one of the most curious documents in the history of morals, is given entire. Franklin's activity as a citizen of Philadelphia is illustrated by two extracts entitled " Public Affairs" and " Civic Pride"— although the reader should remember that there are no headings or chapter divisions in the original. The account of his singular friendship with George Whitefield is reprinted in full, and there are two brief passages relating to the famous Franklin stove and to the Doctor's experiments with electricity.

Of the literary value of the " Autobiography" but little need be said. Its ease and originality, its humor, its combination of shrewd worldliness and overflowing benevolence, have long since given it a place among the great autobiographies. Franklin's own manuscript, it may be added, after surviving singular vicissitudes of fortune, was printed for the first time in 1868, under the editorship of Mr. John Bigelow. This text, differing in many points from the one originally published by William Temple Franklin in 1817, and preserving Franklin's occasionally inconsistent spelling, has been here reprinted by permission.

The text of " Poor Richard's Almanac," likewise, is believed to be an accurate reproduction of the edition of 1757, which threw into connected form the proverbial sayings that for many years had given spice to Franklin's annual " Almanacs." The motive that led him to

Introduction

the collection and publication of these curt, wise comments upon life and the world is described in the "Autobiography," in a passage here printed as an introductory note to the "Almanac." Franklin's account of the contemporary influence of "Poor Richard" is no whit exaggerated. Mr. John T. Morse, Jr., one of Franklin's recent biographers, says: "'Poor Richard' was the revered and popular schoolmaster of a young nation during its period of tutelage. His teachings are among the powerful forces which have gone to shaping the habits of Americans. His terse and picturesque bits of the wisdom and the virtue of this world are familiar in our mouths to-day ; they moulded our great-grandparents and their children ; they have informed our popular traditions ; they still influence our actions, guide our ways of thinking, and establish our points of view, with the constant control of acquired habits which we little suspect."

The shrewd wit that was the salt of the "Almanac" characterizes also Franklin's essays and miscellaneous writings. They are models of an effective popular style that loses no dignity in becoming colloquial. Carelessly as Franklin often wrote, his acquaintance with the best English prose and a happy instinct that was quite his own kept him as far from affectation as from dulness. His story of "The Whistle" is perhaps the most famous of these compositions, but they are all delightful.

Introduction

Nothing could be more perfect of its kind than Franklin's speech in the Federal Convention of 1787, in favor of opening its daily sessions with prayer. It is decorous, eloquent, irreproachable. Yet it seems to have convinced but very few members of the Convention, and in truth Franklin's real attitude toward that other world whose assistance he then entreated is difficult to determine with any certainty. He was not " spiritually-minded "—as his friend Whitefield would have understood that phrase. Yet he sought virtue persistently, and in spite of early " errata " the printer's life was governed by noble impulses and guided to worthy ends. One of the ablest men of his century, he was also one of the most useful.

Readers of this little volume will miss the story of Franklin the patriot, the diplomatist, the statesman ; they will have merely a glimpse of the scientist ; but the temper of the man is revealed upon every page. It is betrayed in his casual letters : in the lines about " prudential algebra " to Dr. Priestley ; in the familiar, " You are my enemy, and I am Yours," to his friend Strahan the printer ; in the admiring, generous sentences addressed to George Washington ; in the account of his peaceful closing years written to his old companion, the Bishop of St. Asaph's. Franklin lived happily and died content, assured of the respect and gratitude of mankind. " Take one thing with another," he wrote to his sister, " and the world is a pretty

Introduction

good sort of a world, and it is our duty to make the best of it and be thankful." That is a more cheery philosophy than modern men of letters have uniformly possessed, yet it remains to be proved that pessimism is a valuable equipment for the pursuit of literature. We have had plenty of gloomy, stormy geniuses since Franklin's day, but we have had very few men who could write a better page of English prose.

BLISS PERRY.

CONTENTS

Autobiography of Benjamin Franklin.

Autobiography of Benjamin Franklin.

Early Life.

TWYFORD, *at the Bishop of St. Asaph's*, 1771.

DEAR SON : I have ever had pleasure in obtaining any little anecdotes of my ancestors. You may remember the inquiries I made among the remains of my relations when you were with me in England, and the journey I undertook for that purpose. Imagining it may be equally agreeable to you to know the circumstances of my life, many of which you are yet unacquainted with, and expecting the enjoyment of a week's uninterrupted leisure in my present country retirement, I sit down to write them for you. To which I have besides some other inducements. Having emerged from the poverty and obscurity in which I was born and bred, to a state of affluence and some degree of reputation in the world, and having gone so far through life with a considerable share of felicity, the conducing means I made use of, which with the blessing of God so well suc-

ceeded, my posterity may like to know, as
they may find some of them suitable to their
own situations, and therefore fit to be imitated.

That felicity, when I reflected on it, has induced me sometimes to say, that were it offered
to my choice, I should have no objection to a
repetition of the same life from its beginning,
only asking the advantages authors have in a
second edition to correct some faults of the
first. So I might, besides correcting the faults,
change some sinister accidents and events of it
for others more favorable. But though this
were denied, I should still accept the offer.
Since such a repetition is not to be expected,
the next thing like living one's life over again
seems to be a recollection of that life, and to
make that recollection as durable as possible by
putting it down in writing.

Hereby, too, I shall indulge the inclination
so natural in old men, to be talking of themselves and their own past actions ; and I shall
indulge it without being tiresome to others,
who, through respect to age, might conceive
themselves obliged to give me a hearing, since
this may be read or not as any one pleases.
And, lastly (I may as well confess it, since my
denial of it will be believed by nobody), perhaps
I shall a good deal gratify my own *vanity*.
Indeed, I scarce ever heard or saw the introductory words, " *Without vanity, I may say,*"
etc., but some vain thing immediately followed.

Early Life

Most people dislike vanity in others, whatever share they may have of it themselves ; but I give it fair quarter wherever I meet with it, being persuaded that it is often productive of good to the possessor, and to others that are within his sphere of action ; and therefore, in many cases, it would not be altogether absurd if a man were to thank God for his vanity among the other comforts of life.

And now I speak of thanking God, I desire with all humility to acknowledge that I owe the mentioned happiness of my past life to His kind providence, which led me to the means I used and gave them success. My belief of this induces me to *hope*, though I must not *presume*, that the same goodness will still be exercised toward me, in continuing that happiness, or enabling me to bear a fatal reverse, which I may experience as others have done ; the complexion of my future fortune being known to Him only in whose power it is to bless to us even our afflictions.

The notes one of my uncles (who had the same kind of curiosity in collecting family anecdotes) once put into my hands, furnished me with several particulars relating to our ancestors. From these notes I learned that the family had lived in the same village, Ecton, in Northamptonshire, for three hundred years, and how much longer he knew not (perhaps from the time when the name of Franklin, that before was the name of an order of people, was assumed by them as a surname when others took surnames all over the kingdom), on a freehold of about thirty acres, aided by the smith's business, which had continued in the family till his time, the eldest son being always bred to that business ; a custom which he and my father followed as to their eldest sons. When I searched the registers at Ecton, I found an account of their births, marriages, and burials from the year 1555 only, there being no registers kept in that parish at any time preceding. By that register I perceived that I was the youngest son of the youngest son for five generations back. My grandfather Thomas, who was born in 1598, lived at Ecton till he grew too old to follow business longer, when he went to live with his son John, a dyer at Banbury, in Oxfordshire, with whom my father served an apprenticeship. There my grandfather died and lies buried. We saw his gravestone in 1758. His eldest son Thomas lived in the house at Ecton, and left it with the land to his only child, a daughter, who, with her husband, one Fisher, of Wellingborough, sold it to Mr. Isted, now lord of the manor there. My grandfather had four sons that grew up, viz.: Thomas, John, Benjamin, and Josiah. I will give you what account I can of them, at this distance from my papers, and if these are not lost in my absence, you will among them find many more particulars.

Thomas was bred a smith under his father ;

but, being ingenious, and encouraged in learning (as all my brothers were) by an Esquire Palmer, then the principal gentleman in that parish, he qualified himself for the business of scrivener ; became a considerable man in the county ; was a chief mover of all public-spirited undertakings for the county or town of Northampton, and his own village, of which many instances were related of him ; and much taken notice of and patronized by the then Lord Halifax. He died in 1702, January 6, old style, just four years to a day before I was born. The account we received of his life and character from some old people at Ecton, I remember, struck you as something extraordinary, from its similarity to what you knew of mine. "Had he died on the same day," you said, "one might have supposed a transmigration."

John was bred a dyer, I believe, of woollens. Benjamin was bred a silk dyer, serving an apprenticeship at London. He was an ingenious man. I remember him well, for when I was a boy he came over to my father in Boston, and lived in the house with us some years. He lived to a great age. His grandson, Samuel Franklin, now lives in Boston. He left behind him two quarto volumes, MS., of his own poetry, consisting of little occasional pieces addressed to his friends and relations. He had formed a short-hand of his own, which he taught me, but, never practising it, I have now forgot it. I was named after this uncle, there being a particular affection between him and my father. He was very pious, a great attender of sermons of the best preachers, which he took down in his short-hand, and had with him many volumes of them. He was also much of a politician ; too much, perhaps, for his station. There fell lately into my hands, in London, a collection he had made of all the principal pamphlets relating to public affairs, from 1641 to 1717 ; many of the volumes are wanting as appears by the numbering, but there still remain eight volumes in folio, and twenty-four in quarto and octavo. A dealer in old books met with them, and knowing me by my sometimes buying of him, he brought them to me. It seems my uncle must have left them here when he went to America, which was above fifty years since. There are many of his notes in the margins.

This obscure family of ours was early in the Reformation, and continued Protestants through the reign of Queen Mary, when they were sometimes in danger of trouble on account of their zeal against popery. They had got an English Bible, and to conceal and secure it, it was fastened open with tapes under and within the cover of a joint-stool. When my great-great-grandfather read it to his family, he turned up the joint-stool upon his knees, turning over the leaves then under the tapes. One of the children stood at the door to give notice if he saw the apparitor coming, who was an officer of the spiritual court. In that case the stool was turned down again upon its feet, when the Bible remained concealed under it as before. This anecdote I had from my uncle Benjamin. The family continued all of the Church of England till about the end of Charles the Second's reign, when some of the ministers that had been outed for non-conformity holding conventicles in Northamptonshire, Benjamin and Josiah adhered to them, and so continued all their lives : the rest of the family remained with the Episcopal Church.

Josiah, my father, married young, and carried his wife with three children into New England, about 1682. The conventicles having been forbidden by law, and frequently disturbed, induced some considerable men of his acquaintance to remove to that country, and he was prevailed with to accompany them thither, where they expected to enjoy their mode of religion with freedom. By the same wife he had four children more born there, and by a second wife ten more, in all seventeen ; of which I remember thirteen sitting at one time at his table, who all grew up to be men and women, and married ; I was the youngest son, and the youngest child but two, and was born in Boston, New England. My mother, the second wife, was Abiah Folger, daughter of Peter Folger, one of the first settlers of New England, of whom honorable mention is made by Cotton Mather, in his church history of that

country, entitled "Magnalia Christi Ameri-
cana," as "*a goodly, learned Englishman*,"
if I remember the words rightly. I have heard
that he wrote sundry small occasional pieces,
but only one of them was printed, which I saw
now many years since. It was written in 1675,
in the home-spun verse of that time and people, and addressed to those then concerned in
the government there. It was in favor of liberty of conscience, and in behalf of the Bap-
tists, Quakers, and other sectaries that had been
under persecution, ascribing the Indian wars,
and other distresses that had befallen the country, to that persecution, as so many judgments
of God to punish so heinous an offense, and ex-
horting a repeal of those uncharitable laws.
The whole appeared to me as written with a
good deal of decent plainness and manly freedom. The six concluding lines I remember,
though I have forgotten the two first of the
stanza ; but the purport of them was, that his
censures proceeded from good-will, and, therefore, he would be known to be the author.

> "Because to be a libeller (says he)
>   I hate it with my heart ;
> From Sherburne town, where now I dwell,
>   My name I do put here ;
> Without offense your real friend,
>   It is Peter Folgier."

My elder brothers were all put apprentices to
different trades. I was put to the grammar-
school at eight years of age, my father intend-

ing to devote me, as the tithe of his sons, to the service of the Church. My early readiness in learning to read (which must have been very early, as I do not remember when I could not read), and the opinion of all his friends, that I should certainly make a good scholar, encouraged him in this purpose of his. My uncle Benjamin, too, approved of it, and proposed to give me all his short-hand volumes of sermons, I suppose as a stock to set up with, if I would learn his character. I continued, however, at the grammar-school not quite one year, though in that time I had risen gradually from the middle of the class of that year to be the head of it, and farther was removed into the next class above it, in order to go with that into the third at the end of the year. But my father in the meantime, from a view of the expense of a college education, which having so large a family he could not well afford, and the mean living many so educated were afterwards able to obtain—reasons that he gave to his friends in my hearing,—altered his first intention, took me from the grammar-school, and sent me to a school for writing and arithmetic, kept by a then famous man, Mr. George Brownell, very successful in his profession generally, and that by mild, encouraging methods. Under him I acquired fair writing pretty soon, but I failed in the arithmetic, and made no progress in it. At ten years old I was taken home to assist my father in his business, which was that of a tal-

low-chandler and soap-boiler, a business he was
not bred to, but had assumed on his arrival in
New England, and on finding his dying trade
would not maintain his family, being in little
request. Accordingly, I was employed in cut-
ting wick for the candles, filling the dipping
mold and the molds for cast candles, attending
the shop, going of errands, etc.

I disliked the trade, and had a strong inclination for the sea, but my father declared against
it ; however, living near the water, I was much
in and about it, learnt early to swim well and
to manage boats ; and when in a boat or canoe
with other boys I was commonly allowed to
govern, especially in any case of difficulty ; and
upon other occasions I was generally a leader
among the boys, and sometimes led them into
scrapes, of which I will mention one instance,
as it shows an early projecting public spirit,
though not then justly conducted.

There was a salt-marsh that bounded part of
the mill-pond, on the edge of which, at high
water, we used to stand to fish for minnows.
By much trampling we had made it a mere
quagmire. My proposal was to build a wharf
there fit for us to stand upon, and I showed my
comrades a large heap of stones which were intended for a new house near the marsh, and
which would very well suit our purpose. Accordingly, in the evening, when the workmen
were gone, I assembled a number of my play-
fellows, and working with them diligently like

Early Life

so many emmets, sometimes two or three to a
stone, we brought them all away and built our
little wharf. The next morning the workmen
were surprised at missing the stones, which
were found in our wharf. Inquiry was made
after the removers ; we were discovered and
complained of ; several of us were corrected by
our fathers ; and, though I pleaded the useful-
ness of the work, mine convinced me that nothing was useful which was not honest.

I think you may like to know something of
his person and character. He had an excellent
constitution of body, was of middle stature,
but well set, and very strong ; he was ingenious, could draw prettily, was skilled a little in
music, and had a clear, pleasing voice, so that
when he played psalm tunes on his violin and
sung withal, as he sometimes did in an evening
after the business of the day was over, it was
extremely agreeable to hear. He had a me-
chanical genius, too, and on occasion was very
handy in the use of other tradesmen's tools ;
but his great excellence lay in a sound understanding and solid judgment in prudential matters, both in private and publick affairs. In
the latter, indeed, he was never employed, the
numerous family he had to educate and the
straitness of his circumstances keeping him
close to his trade ; but I remember well his
being frequently visited by leading people, who
consulted him for his opinion in affairs of the
town or of the church he belonged to, and

showed a good deal of respect for his judgment and advice ; he was also much consulted by private persons about their affairs when any difficulty occurred, and frequently chosen an arbitrator between contending parties. At his table he liked to have as often as he could some sensible friend or neighbor to converse with, and always took care to start some ingenious or useful topic for discourse, which might tend to improve the minds of his children. By this means he turned our attention to what was good, just, and prudent in the conduct of life, and little or no notice was ever taken of what related to the victuals on the table, whether it was well or ill dressed, in or out of season, of good or bad flavor, preferable or inferior to this or that other thing of the kind, so that I was bro't up in such a perfect inattention to those matters as to be quite indifferent what kind of food was set before me, and so unobservant of it, that to this day if I am asked I can scarce tell a few hours after dinner what I dined upon. This has been a convenience to me in travelling, where my companions have been sometimes very unhappy for want of a suitable gratification of their more delicate, because better instructed, tastes and appetites.

My mother had likewise an excellent constitution ; she suckled all her ten children. I never knew either my father or mother to have any sickness but that of which they died, he at 89, and she at 85 years of age. They lie buried together at Boston, where I some years since placed a marble over their grave, with this inscription :

JOSIAH FRANKLIN,
and
ABIAH his wife,
lie here interred.
They lived lovingly together in wedlock
fifty-five years.
Without an estate, or any gainful employment,
By constant labor and industry,
with God's blessing,
They maintained a large family
comfortably,
and brought up thirteen children
and seven grandchildren
reputably.
From this instance, reader,
Be encouraged to diligence in thy calling,
And distrust not Providence.
He was a pious and prudent man ;
She, a discreet and virtuous woman.
Their youngest son,
In filial regard to their memory,
Places this stone.
J. F. born 1655, died 1744, Ætat 89.
A. F. born 1667, died 1752, —— 85.

By my rambling digressions I perceive myself to be grown old. I us'd to write more methodically. But one does not dress for private company as for a public ball. 'T is perhaps only negligence.

To return : I continued thus employed in my father's business for two years, that is, till I was twelve years old ; and my brother John, who was bred to that business, having left my father, married, and set up for himself at Rhode Island, there was all appearance that I was destined to supply his place, and become a tallow-chandler. But my dislike to the trade continuing, my father was under apprehensions that if he did not find one for me more agreeable, I should break away and get to sea, as his son Josiah had done, to his great vexation. He therefore sometimes took me to walk with him, and see joiners, bricklayers, turners, braziers, etc., at their work, that he might observe my inclination, and endeavor to fix it on some trade or other on land. It has ever since been a pleasure to me to see good workmen handle their tools ; and it has been useful to me, having learnt so much by it as to be able to do little jobs myself in my house when a workman could not readily be got, and to construct little machines for my experiments, while the intention of making the experiment was fresh and warm in my mind. My father at last fixed upon the cutler's trade, and my uncle Benjamin's son Samuel, who was bred to that business in London, being about that time established in Boston, I was sent to be with him some time on liking. But his expectations of a fee with me displeasing my father, I was taken home again.

From a child I was fond of reading, and all the little money that came into my hands was ever laid out in books. Pleased with the Pilgrim's Progress, my first collection was of John Bunyan's works in separate little volumes. I afterward sold them to enable me to buy R. Burton's Historical Collections ; they were small chapmen's books, and cheap, 40 or 50 in all. My father's little library consisted chiefly of books in polemic divinity, most of which I read, and have since often regretted that, at a time when I had such a thirst for knowledge, more proper books had not fallen in my way, since it was now resolved I should not be a clergyman. Plutarch's Lives there was in which I read abundantly, and I still think that time spent to great advantage. There was also a book of De Foe's, called an Essay on Projects, and another of Dr. Mather's, called Essays to do Good, which perhaps gave me a turn of thinking that had an influence on some of the principal future events of my life.

This bookish inclination at length determined my father to make me a printer, though he had already one son (James) of that profession. In 1717 my brother James returned from England with a press and letters to set up his business in Boston. I liked it much better than that of my father, but still had a hankering for the sea. To prevent the apprehended effect of such an inclination, my father was impatient to have me bound to my brother. I stood out some time, but at last was persuaded and signed the indentures when I was yet but twelve years old. I was to serve as an apprentice till I was twenty-one years of age, only I was to be allowed journeyman's wages during the last year. In a little time I made great proficiency in the business, and became a useful hand to my brother. I now had access to better books. An acquaintance with the apprentices of booksellers enabled me sometimes to borrow a small one, which I was careful to return soon and clean. Often I sat up in my room reading the greatest part of the night, when the book was borrowed in the evening and to be returned early in the morning, lest it should be missed or wanted.

And after some time an ingenious tradesman, Mr. Matthew Adams, who had a pretty collection of books, and who frequented our printing-house, took notice of me, invited me to his library, and very kindly lent me such books as I chose to read. I now took a fancy to poetry, and made some little pieces ; my brother, thinking it might turn to account, encouraged me, and put me on composing occasional ballads. One was called " The Lighthouse Tragedy," contained an account of the drowning of Captain Worthilake, with his two daughters : the other was a sailor's song, on the taking of *Teach* (or Blackbeard) the pirate. They were wretched stuff, in the Grub-street-ballad style ; and when they were printed he sent me about the town to sell them. The first sold wonderfully, the event being recent, having made a great noise. This flattered my vanity ; but my father discouraged me by ridiculing my performances, and telling me verse-makers were generally beggars. So I escaped being a poet, most probably a very bad one ; but as prose writing has been of great use to me in the course of my life, and was a principal means of my advancement, I shall tell you how, in such a situation, I acquired what little ability I have in that way.

There was another bookish lad in the town, John Collins by name, with whom I was intimately acquainted. We sometimes disputed, and very fond we were of argument, and very desirous of confuting one another, which disputatious turn, by the way, is apt to become a very bad habit, making people often extremely disagreeable in company by the contradiction that is necessary to bring it into practice ; and thence, besides souring and spoiling the conversation, is productive of disgusts and, perhaps, enmities where you may have occasion for friendship. I had caught it by reading my father's books of dispute about religion. Persons of good sense, I have since observed, seldom fall into it, except lawyers, university men, and men of all sorts that have been bred at Edinborough.

A question was once, somehow or other, started between Collins and me, of the propriety of educating the female sex in learning, and their abilities for study. He was of opinion that it was improper, and that they were naturally unequal to it. I took the contrary side, perhaps a little for dispute's sake. He was naturally more eloquent, had a ready plenty of words ; and sometimes, as I thought, bore me down more by his fluency than by the strength of his reasons. As we parted without

settling the point, and were not to see one another again for some time, I sat down to put
my arguments in writing, which I copied fair
and sent to him. He answered, and I replied.
Three or four letters of a side had passed, when
my father happened to find my papers and read
them. Without entering into the discussion,
he took occasion to talk to me about the manner
of my writing ; observed that, though I had
the advantage of my antagonist in correct spelling and pointing (which I ow'd to the printing-
house), I fell far short in elegance of expression,
in method and in perspicuity, of which he convinced me by several instances. I saw the justice of his remarks and thence grew more atten-
tive to the manner in writing, and determined
to endeavor at improvement.

About this time I met with an odd volume of
the *Spectator*. It was the third. I had never
before seen any of them. I bought it, read it
over and over, and was much delighted with
it. I thought the writing excellent, and wished,
if possible, to imitate it. With this view I took
some of the papers, and, making short hints of
the sentiment in each sentence, laid them by a
few days, and then, without looking at the
book, try'd to compleat the papers again, by
expressing each hinted sentiment at length,
and as fully as it had been expressed before, in
any suitable words that should come to hand.
Then I compared my *Spectator* with the original, discovered some of my faults, and cor-

rected them. But I found I wanted a stock of words, or a readiness in recollecting and using them, which I thought I should have acquired before that time if I had gone on making verses ; since the continual occasion for words of the same import, but of different length, to suit the measure, or of different sound for the rhyme, would have laid me under a constant necessity of searching for variety, and also have tended to fix that variety in my mind, and make me master of it. Therefore I took some of the tales and turned them into verse ; and, after a time, when I had pretty well forgotten the prose, turned them back again. I also sometimes jumbled my collections of hints into confusion, and after some weeks endeavored to reduce them into the best order, before I began to form the full sentences and compleat the paper. This was to teach me method in the arrangement of thoughts. By comparing my work afterwards with the original, I discovered many faults and amended them ; but I sometimes had the pleasure of fancying that, in certain particulars of small import, I had been lucky enough to improve the method or the language, and this encouraged me to think I might possibly in time come to be a tolerable English writer, of which I was extreamly ambitious. My time for these exercises and for reading was at night, after work or before it began in the morning, or on Sundays, when I contrived to be in the printing-house alone, evading as much as I could the common attendance on public worship which my father used to exact of me when I was under his care, and which indeed I still thought a duty, though I could not, as it seemed to me, afford time to practise it.

When about 16 years of age I happened to meet with a book, written by one Tryon, recommending a vegetable diet. I determined to go into it. My brother, being yet unmarried, did not keep house, but boarded himself and his apprentices in another family. My refusing to eat flesh occasioned an inconveniency, and I was frequently chid for my singularity. I made myself acquainted with Tryon's manner of preparing some of his dishes, such as boiling potatoes or rice, making hasty pudding, and a few others, and then proposed to my brother, that if he would give me, weekly, half the money he paid for my board, I would board myself. He instantly agreed to it, and I presently found that I could save half what he paid me. This was an additional fund for buying books. But I had another advantage in it. My brother and the rest going from the printing-house to their meals, I remained there alone, and, despatching presently my light repast, which often was no more than a biscuit or a slice of bread, a handful of raisins or a tart from the pastry-cook's, and a glass of water, had the rest of the time till their return for study, in which I made the greater progress, from that greater clearness of head and quicker apprehension which usually attend temperance in eating and drinking.

And now it was that, being on some occasion made asham'd of my ignorance in figures, which I had twice failed in learning when at school, I took Cocker's book of Arithmetick, and went through the whole by myself with great ease. I also read Seller's and Shermy's books of Navigation, and became acquainted with the little geometry they contain ; but never proceeded far in that science. And I read about this time Locke " On Human Understanding," and the " Art of Thinking," by Messrs. du Port Royal.

While I was intent on improving my language, I met with an English grammar (I think it was Greenwood's), at the end of which there were two little sketches of the arts of rhetoric and logic, the latter finishing with a specimen of a dispute in the Socratic method ; and soon after I procur'd Xenophon's " Memorable Things of Socrates," wherein there are many instances of the same method. I was charm'd with it, adopted it, dropt my abrupt contradiction and positive argumentation, and put on the humble inquirer and doubter. And being then, from reading Shaftesbury and Collins, become a real doubter in many points of our religious doctrine, I found this method safest for myself and very embarrassing to those against whom I used it ; therefore I took a delight in it, practis'd it continually, and grew very artful and expert in drawing people, even of superior knowledge, into concessions, the consequences of which they did not foresee, entangling them in difficulties out of which they could not extricate themselves, and so obtaining victories that neither myself nor my cause always deserved. I continu'd this method some few years, but gradually left it, retaining only the habit of expressing myself in terms of modest diffidence ; never using, when I advanced any thing that may possibly be disputed, the words *certainly*, *undoubtedly*, or any others that give the air of positiveness to an opinion ; but rather say, I conceive or apprehend a thing to be so and so ; it appears to me, or *I should think it so or so*, for such and such reasons ; or *I imagine it to be so ;* or *it is so, if I am not mistaken.* This habit, I believe, has been of great advantage to me when I have had occasion to inculcate my opinions, and persuade men into measures that I have been from time to time engag'd in promoting ; and, as the chief ends of conversation are to *inform* or to be *informed*, to *please* or to *persuade*, I wish well-meaning, sensible men would not lessen their power of doing good by a positive, assuming manner, that seldom fails to disgust, tends to create opposition, and to defeat every one of those purposes for which speech was given to us, to wit, giving or receiving information or pleasure. For, if you would inform, a positive and dogmatical manner in advancing your sentiments may provoke contradiction and prevent a candid attention. If you wish information and improvement from the knowledge of others, and yet at the same time express yourself as firmly fix'd in your present opinions, modest, sensible men, who do not love disputation, will probably leave you undisturbed in the possession of your error. And by such a manner, you can seldom hope to recommend yourself in *pleasing* your hearers, or to persuade those whose concurrence you desire. Pope says, judiciously :

> " *Men should be taught as if you taught them not,*
> *And things unknown propos'd as things forgot"* ;

farther recommending to us

> " To speak, tho' sure, with seeming diffidence."

And he might have coupled with this line that which he has coupled with another, I think, less properly :

> " For want of modesty is want of sense."

If you ask, Why less properly? I must repeat the lines :

> " Immodest words admit of no defense,
> For want of modesty is want of sense."

Now, is not *want of sense* (where a man is so unfortunate as to want it) some apology for his *want of modesty?* and would not the lines stand more justly thus ?

> " Immodest words admit *but* this defense,
> That want of modesty is want of sense."

This, however, I should submit to better judgments.

My brother had, in 1720 or 1721, begun to print a newspaper. It was the second that appeared in America, and was called the *New England Courant*. The only one before it was the *Boston News-Letter*. I remember his being dissuaded by some of his friends from the undertaking, as not likely to succeed, one newspaper being, in their judgment, enough for America. At this time (1771) there are not less than five-and-twenty. He went on, however, with the undertaking, and after having worked in composing the types and printing off the sheets, I was employed to carry the papers thro' the streets to the customers.

He had some ingenious men among his friends, who amus'd themselves by writing little pieces for this paper, which gain'd it credit and made it more in demand, and these gentlemen often visited us. Hearing their conversations and their accounts of the approbation their papers were received with, I was excited to try my hand among them; but, being still a boy, and suspecting that my brother would object to printing any thing of mine in his paper if he knew it to be mine, I contrived to disguise my hand, and, writing an anonymous paper, I put it in at night under the door of the printing-house. It was found in the morning, and communicated to his writing friends when they call'd in as usual. They read it, commented on it in my hearing, and I had the exquisite pleasure of finding it met with their approbation, and that, in their different guesses at the author, none were named but men of some character among us for learning and ingenuity. I suppose now that I was rather lucky in my judges, and that perhaps they were not really so very good ones as I then esteem'd them.

Encourag'd, however, by this, I wrote and convey'd in the same way to the press several more papers, which were equally approv'd ; and I kept my secret till my small fund of sense for such performances was pretty well exhausted, and then I discovered it, when I began to be considered a little more by my brother's acquaintance, and in a manner that did not quite please him, as he thought, probably with reason, that it tended to make me too vain. And perhaps this might be one occasion of the differences that we began to have about this time. Though a brother, he considered himself as my master, and me as his apprentice, and accordingly expected the same services from me as he would from another, while I thought he demean'd me too much in some he requir'd of me, who from a brother expected more indulgence. Our disputes were often brought before our father, and I fancy I was either generally in the right, or else a better pleader, because the judgment was generally in my favor. But my brother was passionate, and had often beaten me, which I took extreamly amiss ; and, thinking my apprenticeship very tedious, I was continually wishing for some opportunity of shortening it, which at length offered in a manner unexpected.*

One of the pieces in our newspaper on some political point, which I have now forgotten, gave offense to the Assembly. He was taken up, censur'd, and imprison'd for a month, by the Speaker's warrant, I suppose, because he would not discover his author. I too was taken up and examin'd before the council ; but, tho' I did not give them any satisfaction, they content'd themselves with admonishing me, and dismissed me, considering me, perhaps, as an apprentice, who was bound to keep his master's secrets.

During my brother's confinement, which I resented a good deal, notwithstanding our private differences, I had the management of the paper ; and I made bold to give our rulers some rubs in it, which my brother took very kindly, while others began to consider me in an unfavorable light, as a young genius that had a turn for libelling and satyr. My brother's discharge was accompany'd with an order of the House (a very odd one), that "*James Franklin should no longer print the paper called the New England Courant.*"

There was a consultation held in our print-

---

* I fancy his harsh and tyrannical treatment of me might be a means of impressing me with that aversion to arbitrary power that has stuck to me through my whole life.

ing-house among his friends, what he should
do in this case. Some proposed to evade the
order by changing the name of the paper ; but
my brother, seeing inconveniences in that, it
was finally concluded on as a better way, to let
it be printed for the future under the name of
BENJAMIN FRANKLIN ; and to avoid the censure
of the Assembly, that might fall on him as
still printing it by his apprentice, the contri-
vance was that my old indenture should be return'd to me, with a full discharge on the back
of it, to be shown on occasion, but to secure to
him the benefit of my service, I was to sign new
indentures for the remainder of the term, which
were to be kept private. A very flimsy scheme
it was ; however, it was immediately executed,
and the paper went on accordingly, under my
name for several months.

At length, a fresh difference arising between
my brother and me, I took upon me to assert
my freedom, presuming that he would not venture to produce the new indentures. It was
not fair in me to take this advantage, and this
I therefore reckon one of the first errata of my
life ; but the unfairness of it weighed little with
me, when under the impressions of resentment
for the blows his passion too often urged him
to bestow upon me, though he was otherwise
not an ill-natur'd man : perhaps I was too saucy
and provoking.

When he found I would leave him, he took
care to prevent my getting employment in any

other printing-house of the town, by going
round and speaking to every master, who accordingly refus'd to give me work. I then
thought of going to New York, as the nearest
place where there was a printer ; and I was
rather inclin'd to leave Boston when I reflected
that I had already made myself a little obnox-
ious to the governing party, and, from the arbitrary proceedings of the Assembly in my
brother's case, it was likely I might, if I stay'd,
soon bring myself into scrapes ; and farther,
that my indiscrete disputations about religion
began to make me pointed at with horror by
good people as an infidel or atheist. I determin'd on the point, but my father now siding
with my brother, I was sensible that, if I attempted to go openly, means would be used to
prevent me. My friend Collins, therefore, undertook to manage a little for me. He agreed
with the captain of a New York sloop for my
passage, under the notion of my being a young
acquaintance of his, that had got a naughty
girl with child, whose friends would compel
me to marry her, and therefore I could not appear or come away publicly. So I sold some
of my books to raise a little money, was taken
on board privately, and as we had a fair wind,
in three days I found myself in New York, near
300 miles from home, a boy of but 17, without
the least recommendation to, or knowledge of
any person in the place, and with very little
money in my pocket.

Early Life

My inclinations for the sea were by this time worn out, or I might now have gratify'd them. But, having a trade, and supposing myself a pretty good workman, I offer'd my service to the printer in the place, old Mr. William Bradford, who had been the first printer in Pennsylvania, but removed from thence upon the quarrel of George Keith. He could give me no employment, having little to do, and help enough already ; but says he, " My son at Philadelphia has lately lost his principal hand, Aquila Rose, by death ; if you go thither, I believe he may employ you." Philadelphia was a hundred miles further ; I set out, however, in a boat for Amboy, leaving my chest and things to follow me round by sea.

In crossing the bay, we met with a squall that tore our rotten sails to pieces, prevented our getting into the Kill, and drove us upon Long Island. In our way, a drunken Dutchman, who was a passenger too, fell overboard ; when he was sinking, I reached through the water to his shock pate, and drew him up, so that we got him in again. His ducking sobered him a little, and he went to sleep, taking first out of his pocket a book, which he desir'd I would dry for him. It proved to be my old favorite author, Bunyan's Pilgrim's Progress, in Dutch, finely printed on good paper, with copper cuts, a dress better than I had ever seen it wear in its own language. I have since found that it has been translated into most of the languages of Europe, and suppose it has been more generally read than any other book, except perhaps the Bible. Honest John was the first that I know of who mix'd narration and dialogue ; a method of writing very engaging to the reader, who in the most interesting parts finds himself, as it were, brought into the company and present at the discourse. De Foe in his " Crusoe," his " Moll Flanders," " Religious Courtship," " Family Instructor," and other pieces, has imitated it with success ; and Richardson has done the same in his " Pamela," etc.

When we drew near the island, we found it was at a place where there could be no landing, there being a great surff on the stony beach. So we dropt anchor, and swung round towards the shore. Some people came down to the water edge and hallow'd to us, as we did to them ; but the wind was so high, and the surff so loud, that we could not hear so as to understand each other. There were canoes on the shore, and we made signs, and hallow'd that they should fetch us ; but they either did not understand us, or thought it impracticable, so they went away, and night coming on, we had no reme ly but to wait till the wind should abate ; and, in the mean time, the boatman and I concluded to sleep, if we could ; and so crowded into the scuttle, with the Dutchman, who was still wet, and the spray beating over the head of our boat, leak'd through to us, so that we were soon almost as wet as he. In this

Early Life

manner we lay all night, with very little rest ;
but the wind abating the next day, we made a
shift to reach Amboy before night, having been
thirty hours on the water, without victuals, or
any drink but a bottle of filthy rum, the water
we sail'd on being salt.

In the evening I found myself very feverish,
and went in to bed ; but, having read somewhere that cold water drank plentifully was
good for a fever, I follow'd the prescription,
sweat plentifully most of the night, my fever
left me, and in the morning, crossing the ferry,
I proceeded on my journey on foot, having fifty
miles to Burlington, where I was told I should
find boats that would carry me the rest of the
way to Philadelphia.

It rained very hard all the day ; I was thoroughly soak'd, and by noon a good deal tired ;
so I stopt at a poor inn, where I stayed all
night, beginning now to wish that I had never
left home. I cut so miserable a figure, too, that
I found, by the questions ask'd me, I was suspected to be some runaway servant, and in danger of being taken up on that suspicion. However, I proceeded the next day, and got in the
evening to an inn, within eight or ten miles of
Burlington, kept by one Dr. Brown. He en-
tered into conversation with me while I took
some refreshment, and, finding I had read a
little, became very sociable and friendly. Our
acquaintance continu'd as long as he liv'd. He
had been, I imagine, an itinerant doctor, for

there was no town in England, or country in Europe, of which he could not give a very particular account. He had some letters, and was ingenious, but much of an unbeliever, and wickedly undertook, some years after, to travestie the Bible in doggrel verse, as Cotton had done Virgil. By this means he set many of the facts in a very ridiculous light, and might have hurt weak minds if his work had been published ; but it never was.

At his house I lay that night, and the next morning reach'd Burlington, but had the mortification to find that the regular boats were gone a little before my coming, and no other expected to go before Tuesday, this being Saturday ; wherefore I returned to an old woman in the town, of whom I had bought gingerbread to eat on the water, and ask'd her advice. She invited me to lodge at her house till a passage by water should offer ; and being tired with my foot travelling, I accepted the invitation. She understanding I was a printer, would have had me stay at that town and follow my business, being ignorant of the stock necessary to begin with. She was very hospitable, gave me a dinner of ox-cheek with great good will, accepting only of a pot of ale in return ; and I thought myself fixed till Tuesday should come. However, walking in the evening by the side of the river, a boat came by, which I found was going towards Philadelphia, with several people in her. They took me in, and, as there was

Early Life

no wind, we row'd all the way ; and about midnight, not having yet seen the city, some of the company were confident we must have passed it, and would row no farther ; the others knew not where we were ; so we put toward the shore, got into a creek, landed near an old fence, with the rails of which we made a fire, the night being cold, in October, and there we remained till daylight. Then one of the company knew the place to be Cooper's Creek, a little above Philadelphia, which we saw as soon as we got out of the creek, and arriv'd there about eight or nine o'clock on the Sunday morning, and landed at the Market-street wharf.

I have been the more particular in this description of my journey, and shall be so of my first entry into that city, that you may in your mind compare such unlikely beginnings with the figure I have since made there. I was in my working dress, my best cloaths being to come round by sea. I was dirty from my journey ; my pockets were stuff'd out with shirts and stockings, and I knew no soul nor where to look for lodging. I was fatigued with travelling, rowing and want of rest, I was very hungry ; and my whole stock of cash consisted of a Dutch dollar, and about a shilling in copper. The latter I gave the people of the boat for my passage, who at first refus'd it, on account of my rowing ; but I insisted on their taking it. A man being sometimes more generous when he has but a little money than when he has plenty, perhaps thro' fear of being thought to have but little.

Then I walked up the street, gazing about till near the market-house I met a boy with bread. I had made many a meal on bread, and, inquiring where he got it, I went immediately to the baker's he directed me to, in Second-street, and ask'd for biscuit, intending such as we had in Boston ; but they, it seems, were not made in Philadelphia. Then I asked for a three-penny loaf, and was told they had none such. So not considering or knowing the difference of money, and the greater cheapness nor the names of his bread, I bade him give me three-penny worth of any sort. He gave me, accordingly, three great puffy rolls. I was surpris'd at the quantity, but took it, and, having no room in my pockets, walk'd off with a roll under each arm, and eating the other. Thus I went up Market-street as far as Fourth-street, passing by the door of Mr. Read, my future wife's father ; when she, standing at the door, saw me, and thought I made, as I certainly did, a most awkward, ridiculous appearance. Then I turned and went down Chestnut-street and part of Walnut-street, eating my roll all the way, and, coming round, found myself again at Market-street wharf, near the boat I came in, to which 1 went for a draught of the river water ; and, being filled with one of my rolls, gave the other two to a woman and her child that came down the river in the boat with us, and were waiting to go farther.

Thus refreshed, I walked again up the street, which by this time had many clean-dressed people in it, who were all walking the same way. I joined them, and thereby was led into the great meeting-house of the Quakers near the market. I sat down among them, and, after looking round awhile and hearing nothing said, being very drowsy thro' labor and want of rest the preceding night, I fell fast asleep, and continu'd so till the meeting broke up, when one was kind enough to rouse me. This was, therefore, the first house I was in, or slept in, in Philadelphia.

Walking down again toward the river, and, looking in the faces of people, I met a young Quaker man, whose countenance I lik'd, and, accosting him, requested he would tell me where a stranger could get lodging. We were then near the sign of the Three Mariners. "Here," says he, "is one place that entertains strangers, but it is not a reputable house; if thee wilt walk with me I 'll show thee a better." He brought me to the Crooked Billet, in Water-street. Here I got a dinner; and, while I was eating it, several sly questions were asked me, as it seemed to be suspected from my youth and appearance that I might be some runaway.

After dinner my sleepiness return'd, and being shown to a bed, I lay down without undressing, and slept till six in the evening, was call'd to supper, went to bed again very early, and slept soundly till next morning. Then I made myself as tidy as I could, and went to Andrew Bradford the printer's. I found in the shop the old man his father, whom I had seen at New York, and who, travelling on horse-back, had got to Philadelphia before me. He introduc'd me to his son, who receiv'd me civ-illy, gave me a breakfast, but told me he did not at present want a hand, being lately sup-pli'd with one ; but there was another printer in town, lately set up, one Keimer, who, per-haps, might employ me ; if not, I should be welcome to lodge at his house, and he would give me a little work to do now and then till fuller business should offer.

The old gentleman said he would go with me to the new printer ; and when we found him, " Neighbor," says Bradford, " I have brought to see you a young man of your business ; per-haps you may want such a one." He ask'd me a few questions, put a composing stick in my hand to see how I work'd, and then said he would employ me soon, though he had just then nothing for me to do ; and, taking old Brad-ford, whom he had never seen before, to be one of the townspeople that had a good will for him, enter'd into a conversation on his present undertaking and prospects ; while Bradford, not discovering that he was the other printer's father, on Keimer's saying he expected soon to get the greatest part of the business into his own hands, drew him on by artful questions, and starting little doubts, to explain all his views, what interest he reli'd on, and in what manner he intended to proceed. I, who stood by and heard all, saw immediately that one of them was a crafty old sophister, and the other a mere novice. Bradford left me with Keimer, who was greatly surpris'd when I told him who the old man was.

Keimer's printing-house, I found, consisted of an old shatter'd press and one small, worn-out font of English, which he was then using himself, composing an Elegy on Aquila Rose, before mentioned, an ingenious young man, of excellent character, much respected in the town, clerk of the Assembly, and a pretty poet. Keimer made verses too, but very indifferently. He could not be said to write them, for his manner was to compose them in the types directly out of his head. So there being no copy, but one pair of cases, and the Elegy likely to require all the letter, no one could help him. I endeavor'd to put his press (which he had not yet us'd, and of which he understood nothing) into order fit to be work'd with ; and promising to come and print off his Elegy as soon as he should have got it ready, I return'd to Bradford's, who gave me a little job to do for the present, and there I lodged and dieted. A few days after, Keimer sent for me to print off the Elegy. And now he had got another pair of cases, and a pamphlet to reprint, on which he set me to work.

These two printers I found poorly qualified for their business. Bradford had not been bred to it, and was very illiterate ; and Keimer, tho' something of a scholar, was a mere compositor, knowing nothing of press-work. He had been one of the French prophets, and could act their enthusiastic agitations. At this time he did not profess any particular religion, but something of all on occasion ; was very ignorant of the world, and had, as I afterward found, a good deal of the knave in his composition. He did not like my lodging at Bradford's while I work'd with him. He had a house, indeed, but without furniture, so he could not lodge me ; but he got me a lodging at Mr. Read's, before mentioned, who was the owner of his house ; and, my chest and clothes being come by this time, I made rather a more respectable appearance in the eyes of Miss Read than I had done when she first happen'd to see me eating my roll in the street.

I began now to have some acquaintance among the young people of the town, that were lovers of reading, with whom I spent my evenings very pleasantly ; and gaining money by my industry and frugality, I lived very agreeably, forgetting Boston as much as I could, and not desiring that any there should know where I resided, except my friend Collins, who was in my secret, and kept it when I wrote to him.

Early Life

At length an incident happened that sent me back again much sooner than I had intended. I had a brother-in-law, Robert Holmes, master of a sloop that traded between Boston and Delaware. He being at Newcastle, forty miles below Philadelphia, heard there of me, and wrote me a letter mentioning the concern of my friends in Boston at my abrupt departure, assuring me of their good will to me, and that every thing would be accommodated to my mind if I would return, to which he exhorted me very earnestly. I wrote an answer to his letter, thank'd him for his advice, but stated my reasons for quitting Boston fully and in such a light as to convince him I was not so wrong as he had apprehended.

Sir William Keith, governor of the province, was then at Newcastle, and Captain Holmes, happening to be in company with him when my letter came to hand, spoke to him of me, and show'd him the letter. The governor read it, and seem'd surpris'd when he was told my age. He said I appear'd a young man of promising parts, and therefore should be encouraged ; the printers at Philadelphia were wretched ones ; and, if I would set up there, he made no doubt I should succeed ; for his part, he would procure me the public business, and do me every other service in his power. This my brother-in-law afterward told me in Boston, but I knew as yet nothing of it ; when, one day, Keimer and I being at work together near the window, we saw the governor and another gentleman (which proved to be Colonel French, of Newcastle), finely dress'd, come directly across the street to our house, and heard them at the door.

Keimer ran down immediately, thinking it a visit to him ; but the governor inquir'd for me, came up, and with a condescension and politeness I had been quite unus'd to, made me many compliments, desired to be acquainted with me, blam'd me kindly for not having made myself known to him when I first came to the place, and would have me away with him to the tavern, where he was going with Colonel French to taste, as he said, some excellent Madeira. I was not a little surpris'd, and Keimer star'd like a pig poison'd. I went, however, with the governor and Colonel French to a tavern, at the corner of Third-street, and over the Madeira he propos'd my setting up my business, laid before me the probabilities of success, and both he and Colonel French assur'd me I should have their interest and influence in procuring the public business of both governments. On my doubting whether my father would assist me in it, Sir William said he would give me a letter to him, in which he would state the advantages, and he did not doubt of prevailing with him. So it was concluded I should return to Boston in the first vessel, with the governor's letter recommending me to my father. In the mean time the intention was to be kept a secret, and I went on working with Keimer as usual, the governor sending for me now and then to dine with him, a very great honor I thought it, and conversing with me in the most affable, familiar, and friendly manner imaginable.

About the end of April, 1724, a little vessel offer'd for Boston. I took leave of Keimer as going to see my friends. The governor gave me an ample letter, saying many flattering things of me to my father, and strongly recommending the project of my setting up at Philadelphia as a thing that must make my fortune. We struck on a shoal in going down the bay, and sprung a leak ; we had a blustering time at sea, and were oblig'd to pump almost continually, at which I took my turn. We arriv'd safe, however, at Boston in about a fortnight. I had been absent seven months, and my friends had heard nothing of me ; for my br. Holmes was not yet return'd, and had not written about me. My unexpected appearance surpris'd the family ; all were, however, very glad to see me, and made me welcome, except my brother. I went to see him at his printing-house. I was better dress'd than ever while in his service, having a genteel new suit from head to foot, a watch, and my pockets lin'd with near five pounds sterling in silver. He receiv'd me not very frankly, look'd me all over, and turn'd to his work again.

The journeymen were inquisitive where I

had been, what sort of a country it was, and how I lik'd it. I prais'd it much, and the happy life I led in it, expressing strongly my intention of returning to it ; and, one of them asking what kind of money we had there, I produc'd a handful of silver, and spread it before them, which was a kind of raree-show they had not been us'd to, paper being the money of Boston. Then I took an opportunity of letting them see my watch ; and, lastly (my brother still grum and sullen), I gave them a piece of eight to drink, and took my leave. This visit of mine offended him extremely ; for, when my mother some time after spoke to him of a reconciliation, and of her wishes to see us on good terms together, and that we might live for the future as brothers, he said I had insulted him in such a manner before his people that he could never forget or forgive it. In this, however, he was mistaken.

My father received the governor's letter with some apparent surprise, but said little of it to me for several days, when Capt. Holmes returning he show'd it to him, ask'd him if he knew Keith, and what kind of man he was ; adding his opinion that he must be of small discretion to think of setting a boy up in business who wanted yet three years of being at man's estate. Holmes said what he could in favor of the project, but my father was clear in the impropriety of it, and at last gave a flat denial to it. Then he wrote a civil letter to Sir William, thanking him for the patronage he had so kindly offered me, but declining to assist me as yet in setting up, I being, in his opinion, too young to be trusted with the management of a business so important, and for which the preparation must be so expensive.

My friend and companion Collins, who was a clerk in the post-office, pleas'd with the account I gave him of my new country, determined to go thither also ; and, while I waited for my father's determination, he set out before me by land to Rhode Island, leaving his books, which were a pretty collection of mathematicks and natural philosophy, to come with mine and me to New York, where he propos'd to wait for me.

My father, tho' he did not approve Sir William's proposition, was yet pleas'd that I had been able to obtain so advantageous a character from a person of such note where I had resided, and that I had been so industrious and careful as to equip myself so handsomely in so short a time ; therefore, seeing no prospect of an accommodation between my brother and me, he gave his consent to my returning again to Philadelphia, advis'd me to behave respectfully to the people there, endeavor to obtain the general esteem, and avoid lampooning and libeling, to which he thought I had too much inclination ; telling me, that by steady industry and a prudent parsimony I might save enough by the time I was one and-twenty to set me up ; and that, if I came near the matter, he would help me out with the rest. This was all I could obtain, except some small gifts as tokens of his and my mother's love, when I embark'd again for New York, now with their approbation and their blessing.

The sloop putting in at Newport, Rhode Island, I visited my brother John, who had been married and settled there some years. He received me very affectionately, for he always lov'd me. A friend of his, one Vernon, having some money due to him in Pennsylvania, about thirty-five pounds currency, desired I would receive it for him, and keep it till I had his directions what to remit it in. Accordingly, he gave me an order. This afterwards occasion'd me a good deal of uneasiness.

At Newport we took in a number of passengers for New York, among which were two young women, companions, and a grave, sensible, matron-like Quaker woman, with her attendants I had shown an obliging readiness to do her some little services, which impress'd her I suppose with a degree of good-will toward me ; therefore, when she saw a daily growing familiarity between me and the two young women, which they appear'd to encourage, she took me aside, and said, " Young man, I am concern'd for thee, as thou has no friend with thee, and seems not to know much of the world, or of the snares youth is expos'd to ; depend upon it, those are very bad women ; I can see it in all their actions ; and if thee art not upon thy guard, they will draw thee into some danger ; they are strangers to thee, and I advise thee, in a friendly concern for thy welfare, to have no acquaintance with them.'' As I seem'd at first not to think so ill of them as she did, she mentioned some things she had observ'd and heard that had escap'd my notice, but now convinc'd me she was right. I thank'd her for her kind advice, and promis'd to follow it. When we arriv'd at New York, they told me where they liv'd, and invited me to come and see them ; but I avoided it, and it was well I did ; for the next day the captain miss'd a silver spoon and some other things, that had been taken out of his cabin, and, knowing that these were a couple of strumpets, he got a warrant to search their lodgings, found the stolen goods, and had the thieves punish'd. So, tho' we had escap'd a sunken rock, which we scrap'd upon in the passage, I thought this escape of rather more importance to me.

At New York I found my friend Collins, who had arriv'd there some time before me. We had been intimate from children, and had read the same books together ; but he had the advantage of more time for reading and studying, and a wonderful genius for mathematical learning, in which he far outstript me. While I liv'd in Boston, most of my hours of leisure for conversation were spent with him, and he continu'd a sober as well as an industrious lad ; was much respected for his learning by several of the clergy and other gentlemen, and seemed to promise making a good figure in life. But, during my absence, he had acquir'd a habit of sotting with brandy ; and I found by his own account, and what I heard from others, that he had been drunk every day since his arrival at New York, and behav'd very oddly. He had gam'd, too, and lost his money, so that I was oblig'd to discharge his lodgings, and defray his expenses to and at Philadelphia, which prov'd extremely inconvenient to me.

The then governor of New York, Burnet (son of Bishop Burnet), hearing from the captain that a young man, one of his passengers, had a great many books, desir'd he would bring me to see him. I waited upon him accordingly, and should have taken Collins with me but that he was not sober. The gov'r. treated me with great civility, show'd me his library, which was a very large one, and we had a good deal of conversation about books and authors. This was the second governor who had done me the honor to take notice of me ; which, to a poor boy like me, was very pleasing.

We proceeded to Philadelphia. I received on the way Vernon's money, without which we could hardly have finish'd our journey. Collins wished to be employ'd in some counting-house ; but, whether they discover'd his dram-ming by his breath, or by his behaviour, tho' he had some recommendations, he met with no success in any application, and continu'd lodging and boarding at the same house with me, and at my expense. Knowing I had that money of Vernon's, he was continually borrowing of me, still promising repayment as soon as he should be in business. At length he had got so much of it that I was distress'd to think what I should do in case of being call'd on to remit it.

His drinking continu'd, about which we sometimes quarrel'd; for, when a little intoxicated, he was very fractious. Once, in a boat on the Delaware with some other young men, he refused to row in his turn. "I will be row'd home," says he. "We will not row you," says I. "You must, or stay all night on the water," says he, "just as you please." The others said, "Let us row; what signifies it?" But, my mind being soured with his other conduct, I continu'd to refuse. So he swore he would make me row, or throw me overboard; and coming along, stepping on the thwarts, toward me, when he came up and struck at me, I clapped my hand under his crutch, and, rising, pitched him head-foremost into the river. I knew he was a good swimmer, and so was under little concern about him; but before he could get round to lay hold of the boat, we had with a few strokes pull'd her out of his reach; and ever when he drew near the boat, we ask'd if he would row, striking a few strokes to slide her away from him. He was ready to die with vexation, and obstinately would not promise to

row. However, seeing him at last beginning
to tire, we lifted him in and brought him home
dripping wet in the evening. We hardly ex-
chang'd a civil word afterwards, and a West
India captain, who had a commission to procure
a tutor for the sons of a gentleman at Barba-
does, happening to meet with him, agreed to
carry him thither. He left me then, promising
to remit me the first money he should receive
in order to discharge the debt ; but I never
heard of him after.

The breaking into this money of Vernon's
was one of the first great errata of my life ; and
this affair show'd that my father was not much
out in his judgment when he suppos'd me too
young to manage business of importance. But
Sir William, on reading his letter, said he was
too prudent. There was great difference in
persons ; and discretion did not always accompany years, nor was youth always without it.
" And since he will not set you up," says he,
" I will do it myself. Give me an inventory of
the things necessary to be had from England,
and I will send for them. You shall repay me
when you are able ; I am resolv'd to have a
good printer here, and I am sure you must succeed." This was spoken with such an appearance of cordiality, that I had not the least doubt
of his meaning what he said. I had hitherto
kept the proposition of my setting up, a secret
in Philadelphia, and I still kept it Had it been
known that I depended on the governor, prob-

ably some friend, that knew him better, would have advis'd me not to rely on him, as I afterwards heard it as his known character to be liberal of promises which he never meant to keep. Yet, unsolicited as he was by me, how could I think his generous offers insincere? I believ'd him one of the best men in the world.

I presented him an inventory of a little printing-house, amounting by my computation to about one hundred pounds sterling. He lik'd it, but ask'd me if my being on the spot in England to choose the types, and see that every thing was good of the kind, might not be of some advantage. "Then," says he, "when there, you may make acquaintances, and establish correspondences in the bookselling and stationery way." I agreed that this might be advantageous. "Then," says he, "get yourself ready to go with *Annis*"; which was the annual ship, and the only one at that time usually passing between London and Philadelphia. But it would be some months before *Annis* sail'd, so I continu'd working with Keimer, fretting about the money Collins had got from me, and in daily apprehensions of being call'd upon by Vernon, which, however, did not happen for some years after.

I believe I have omitted mentioning that, in my first voyage from Boston, being becalm'd off Block Island, our people set about catching cod, and hauled up a good many. Hitherto I had stuck to my resolution of not eating animal food, and on this occasion I consider'd, with my master Tryon, the taking every fish as a kind of unprovoked murder, since none of them had, or ever could do us any injury that might justify the slaughter. All this seemed very reasonable. But I had formerly been a great lover of fish, and, when this came hot out of the frying-pan, it smelt admirably well. I balanc'd some time between principle and inclination, till I recollected that, when the fish were opened, I saw smaller fish taken out of their stomachs ; then thought I, " If you eat one another, I don't see why we may n't eat you." So I din'd upon cod very heartily, and con. tinued to eat with other people, returning only now and then occasionally to a vegetable diet. So convenient a thing it is to be a *reasonable creature*, since it enables one to find or make a reason for every thing one has a mind to do.

Keimer and I liv'd on a pretty good familiar footing, and agreed tolerably well, for he suspected nothing of my setting up. He retained a great deal of his old enthusiasms and lov'd argumentation. We therefore had many disputations. I used to work him so with my Socratic method, and had trepann'd him so often by questions apparently so distant from any point we had in hand, and yet by degrees lead to the point, and brought him into difficulties and contradictions, that at last he grew ridiculously cautious, and would hardly answer me the most common question, without asking first : " *What do you intend to infer from that ?*" However, it gave him so high an opinion of my abilities in the confuting way, that he seriously proposed my being his colleague in a project he had of setting up a new sect. He was to preach the doctrines, and I was to confound all opponents. When he came to explain with me upon the doctrines, I found several conundrums which I objected to, unless I might have my way a little too, and introduce some of mine.

Keimer wore his beard at full length, because somewhere in the Mosaic law it is said, " *Thou shalt not mar the corners of thy beard.*" He likewise kept the Seventh day, Sabbath ; and these two points were essentials with him. I dislik'd both ; but agreed to admit them upon condition of his adopting the doctrine of using no animal food. " I doubt," said he, " my constitution will not bear that." I assur'd him it would, and that he would be better for it. He was usually a great glutton, and I promised myself some diversion in half starving him. He agreed to try the practice, if I would keep him company. I did so, and we held it for three months. We had our victuals dress'd, and brought to us regularly by a woman in the neighborhood, who had from me a list of forty dishes, to be prepar'd for us at different times, in all which there was neither fish, flesh, nor fowl, and the whim suited me the better at this time from the cheapness of it, not costing us above eighteen pence sterling each per week. I have since kept several Lents most strictly, leaving the common diet for that, and that for the common, abruptly, without the least inconvenience, so that I think there is little in the advice of making those changes by easy gradations. I went on pleasantly, but poor Keimer suffered grievously, tired of the project, long'd for the flesh-pots of Egypt, and order'd a roast pig. He invited me and two women friends to dine with him ; but, it being brought too soon upon table, he could not resist the temptation, and ate the whole before we came.

I had made some courtship during this time to Miss Read. I had a great respect and affection for her, and had some reason to believe she had the same for me ; but, as I was about to take a long voyage, and we were both very young, only a little above eighteen, it was thought must prudent by her mother to prevent our going too far at present, as a marriage, if it was to take place, would be more convenient after my return, when I should be, as I expected, set up in my business. Perhaps, too, she thought my expectations not so well founded as I imagined them to be.

My chief acquaintances at this time were Charles Osborne, Joseph Watson, and James Ralph, all lovers of reading. The two first were clerks to an eminent scrivener or conveyancer in the town, Charles Brogden ; the other was clerk to a merchant. Watson was a pious, sensible young man, of great integrity ; the others rather more lax in their principles of religion, particularly Ralph, who, as well as Collins, had been unsettled by me, for which they both made me suffer. Osborne was sensible, candid, frank ; sincere and affectionate to his friends ; but, in literary matters, too fond of criticising. Ralph was ingenious, genteel in his manners, and extremely eloquent ; I think I never knew a prettier talker. Both of them great admirers of poetry, and began to try their hands in little pieces. Many pleasant walks we four had together on Sundays into the woods, near Schuylkill, where we read to one another, and conferr'd on what we read.

Ralph was inclin'd to pursue the study of poetry, not doubting but he might become eminent in it, and make his fortune by it, alleging that the best poets must, when they first began to write, make as many faults as he did. Osborne dissuaded him, assur'd him he had no genius for poetry, and advis'd him to think of nothing beyond the business he was bred to ; that, in the mercantile way, tho' he had no stock, he might, by his diligence and punctuality, recommend himself to employment as a factor, and in time acquire wherewith to trade on his own account. I approv'd the amusing one's self with poetry now and then, so far as to improve one's language, but no farther.

On this it was propos'd that we should each of us, at our next meeting, produce a piece of our own composing, in order to improve by our mutual observations, criticisms, and corrections. As language and expression were what we had in view, we excluded all considerations of invention by agreeing that the task should be a version of the eighteenth Psalm, which describes the descent of Deity. When the time of our meeting grew nigh, Ralph called on me first, and let me know his piece was ready. I told him I had been busy, and, having little inclination, had done nothing. He then show'd me his piece for my opinion, and I much approv'd it, as it appear'd to me to have great merit. "Now," says he, "Osborne never will allow the least merit in any thing of mine, but makes 1000 criticisms out of mere envy. He is not so jealous of you; I wish, therefore, you would take this piece, and produce it as yours; I will pretend not to have had time, and so produce nothing. We shall then see what he will say to it." It was agreed, and I immediately transcrib'd it, that it might appear in my own hand.

We met; Watson's performance was read; there were some beauties in it, but many defects. Osborne's was read; it was much better; Ralph did it justice; remarked some faults, but applauded the beauties. He himself had nothing to produce. I was backward; seemed desirous of being excused; had not had sufficient time to correct, etc.; but no excuse would be admitted; produce I must. It was read and repeated ; Watson and Osborne gave up the contest, and join'd in applauding it. Ralph only made some criticisms, and propos'd some amendments ; but I defended my text. Osborne was against Ralph, and told him he was no better a critic than poet, so he dropt the argument. As the two went home together, Osborne expressed himself still more strongly in favor of what he thought my production ; having restrain'd himself before, as he said, lest I should think it flattery. " But who would have imagin'd," said he, " that Franklin had been capable of such a performance ; such painting, such force, such fire ! He has even improv'd the original. In his common conversation he seems to have no choice of words ; he hesitates and blunders ; and yet, good God ! how he writes !" When we next met, Ralph discovered the trick we had plaid him, and Osborne was a little laught at.

This transaction fixed Ralph in his resolution of becoming a poet. I did all I could to dissuade him from it, but he continued scribbling verses till Pope cured him. He became, however, a pretty good prose writer. More of him hereafter. But, as I may not have occasion again to mention the other two, I shall just remark here, that Watson died in my arms a few years after, much lamented, being the best of our set. Osborne went to the West Indies, where he became an eminent lawyer and made money, but died young. He and I had made a serious agreement, that the one who happen'd first to die should, if possible, make a friendly visit to the other, and acquaint him how he found things in that separate state. But he never fulfill'd his promise.

The governor, seeming to like my company, had me frequently to his house, and his setting me up was always mention'd as a fixed thing. I was to take with me letters recommendatory to a number of his friends, besides the letter of credit to furnish me with the necessary money for purchasing the press and types, paper, etc. For these letters I was appointed to call at different times, when they were to be ready ; but a future time was still named. Thus he went on till the ship, whose departure too had been several times postponed, was on the point of sailing. Then, when I call'd to take my leave and receive the letters, his secretary, Dr. Bard, came out to me and said the governor was extremely busy in writing, but would be down at Newcastle before the ship, and there the letters would be delivered to me.

Ralph, though married, and having one child, had determined to accompany me on this voyage. It was thought he intended to establish a correspondence, and obtain goods to sell on commission ; but I found afterwards, that, thro' some discontent with his wife's relations, he proposed to leave her on their hands, and never return again. Having taken leave of my friends, and interchang'd some promises with

Early Life

Miss Read, I left Philadelphia in the ship, which anchor'd at Newcastle. The governor was there ; but when I went to his lodging, the secretary came to me from him with the civillest message in the world, that he could not then see me, being engaged in business of the utmost importance, but should send the letters to me on board, wish'd me heartily a good voyage and a speedy return, etc. I returned on board a little puzzled, but still not doubting.

Mr. Andrew Hamilton, a famous lawyer of Philadelphia, had taken passage in the same ship for himself and son, and with Mr. Denham, a Quaker merchant, and Messrs. Onion and Russel, masters of an iron work in Maryland, had engag'd the great cabin ; so that Ralph and I were forced to take up with a berth in the steerage, and none on board knowing us, were considered as ordinary persons. But Mr. Hamilton and his son (it was James, since governor) return'd from Newcastle to Philadelphia, the father being recall'd by a great fee to plead for a seized ship ; and, just before we sail'd, Colonel French coming on board, and showing me great respect, I was more taken notice of, and, with my friend Ralph, invited by the other gentlemen to come into the cabin, there being now room. Accordingly, we remov'd thither.

Understanding that Colonel French had brought on board the governor's despatches, I ask'd the captain for those letters that were to be put under my care. He said all were put into the bag together and he could not then come at them ; but, before we landed in England, I should have an opportunity of picking them out ; so I was satisfied for the present, and we proceeded on our voyage. We had a sociable company in the cabin, and lived uncommonly well, having the addition of all Mr. Hamilton's stores, who had laid in plentifully. In this passage Mr. Denham contracted a friendship for me that continued during his life. The voyage was otherwise not a pleasant one, as we had a great deal of bad weather.

When we came into the Channel, the captain kept his word with me, and gave me an opportunity of examining the bag for the governor's letters. I found none* upon which my name was put as under my care. I picked out six or seven, that, by the handwriting, I thought might be the promised letters, especially as one of them was directed to Basket, the king's printer, and another to some stationer. We arriv'd in London the 24th of December, 1724. I waited upon the stationer, who came first in my way, delivering the letter as from Governor Keith. "I don't know such a person," says he ; but, opening the letter, "O! this is from Riddlesden. I have lately found him to be a complete rascal, and I will have nothing to do with him, nor receive any letters from him."

* Evidently intended for "some."—ED.

Early Life

So, putting the letter into my hand, he turn'd
on his heel and left me to serve some customer.
I was surpris'd to find these were not the governor's letters ; and, after recollecting and comparing circumstances, I began to doubt his sincerity.   I found my friend Denham, and opened
the whole affair to him.   He let me into Keith's
character ; told me there was not the least
probability that he had written any letters for
me ; that no one, who knew him, had the smallest dependence on him ; and he laught at the
notion of the governor's giving me a letter of
credit, having, as he said, no credit to give.
On my expressing some concern about what I
should do, he advised me to endeavor getting
some employment in the way of my business.
"Among the printers here," said he, "you will
improve yourself, and when you return to
America, you will set up to greater advantage."

We both of us happened to know, as well as
the stationer, that Riddlesden, the attorney,
was a very knave. He had half ruin'd Miss
Read's father by persuading him to be bound
for him.   By this letter it appear'd there was a
secret scheme on foot to the prejudice of Hamilton (suppos'd to be then coming over with us);
and that Keith was concerned in it with Riddlesden.   Denham, who was a friend of Hamilton's, thought he ought to be acquainted with
it ; so, when he arriv'd in England, which was
soon after, partly from resentment and ill-will
to Keith and Riddlesden, and partly from good-

will to him, I waited on him, and gave him the
letter. He thank'd me cordially, the information being of importance to him ; and from that
time he became my friend, greatly to my advantage afterwards on many occasions.

But what shall we think of a governor's play-
ing such pitiful tricks, and imposing so grossly
on a poor ignorant boy ! It was a habit he had
acquired. He wish'd to please everybody ;
and, having little to give, he gave expectations.
He was otherwise an ingenious, sensible man,
a pretty good writer, and a good governor for
the people, tho' not for his constituents, the
proprietaries, whose instructions he sometimes
disregarded. Several of our best laws were of
his planning and passed during his adminis-
tration.

Ralph and I were inseparable companions.
We took lodgings together in Little Britain at
three shillings and sixpence a week—as much
as we could then afford. He found some relations, but they were poor, and unable to assist
him. He now let me know his intentions of remaining in London, and that he never meant
to return to Philadelphia. He had brought no
money with him, the whole he could muster
having been expended in paying his passage.
I had fifteen pistoles ; so he borrowed occasionally of me to subsist while he was looking out
for business. He first endeavored to get into
the playhouse, believing himself qualify'd for
an actor, but Wilkes, to whom he apply'd, ad-

vis'd him candidly not to think of that employment, as it was impossible he should succeed in
it.   Then he propos'd to Roberts, a publisher
in Paternoster Row, to write for him a weekly
paper like the *Spectator*, on certain conditions,
which Roberts did not approve.   Then he endeavored to get employment as a hackney
writer, to copy for the stationers and lawyers
about the Temple, but could find no vacancy.

I immediately got into work at Palmer's, then
a famous printing-house in Bartholomew Close,
and here I continu'd near a year.   I was pretty
diligent, but spent with Ralph a good deal of
my earnings in going to plays and other places
of amusement.   We had together consumed all
my pistoles, and now just rubbed on from hand
to mouth.   He seem'd quite to forget his wife
and child, and I, by degrees, my engagements
with Miss Read, to whom I never wrote more
than one letter, and that was to let her know I
was not likely soon to return.   This was another of the great errata of my life, which I
should wish to correct if I were to live it over
again.   In fact, by our expenses, I was con-
stantly kept unable to pay my passage.

At Palmer's I was employed in composing
for the second edition of Wollaston's " Religion
of Nature."   Some of his reasonings not ap-
pearing to me well founded, I wrote a little
metaphysical piece in which I made remarks on
them.   It was entitled " Dissertation on Liberty and Necessity, Pleasure and Pain."   I in-

scribed it to my friend Ralph ; I printed a small number. It occasion'd my being more consider'd by Mr. Palmer as a young man of some ingenuity, tho' he seriously expostulated with me upon the principles of my pamphlet, which to him appear'd abominable. My printing this pamphlet was another erratum. While I lodg'd in Little Britain I made an acquaintance with one Wilcox, a bookseller, whose shop was at the next door. He had an immense collection of second-hand books. Circulating libraries were not then in use ; but we agreed that, on certain reasonable terms, which I have now forgotten, I might take, read, and return any of his books. This I esteem'd a great advantage, and I made as much use of it as I could.

My pamphlet by some means falling into the hands of one Lyons, a surgeon, author of a book entitled "The Infallibility of Human Judgment," it occasioned an acquaintance between us. He took great notice of me, called on me often to converse on those subjects, carried me to the Horns, a pale ale house in —— Lane, Cheapside, and introduced me to Dr. Mandeville, author of the " Fable of the Bees," who had a club there, of which he was the soul, being a most facetious, entertaining companion. Lyons, too, introduced me to Dr. Pemberton, at Batson's Coffee-house, who promis'd to give me an opportunity, some time or other, of seeing Sir Isaac Newton, of which I was extremely desirous ; but this never happened.

I had brought over a few curiosities, among which the principal was a purse made of the asbestos, which purifies by fire. Sir Hans Sloane heard of it, came to see me, and invited me to his house in Bloomsbury Square, where he show'd me all his curiosities, and persuaded me to let him add that to the number, for which he paid me handsomely.

In our house there lodg'd a young woman, a milliner, who, I think, had a shop in the Cloisters. She had been genteelly bred, was sensible and lively, and of most pleasing conversation. Ralph read plays to her in the evenings, they grew intimate, she took another lodging, and he followed her. They liv'd together some time ; but, he being still out of business, and her income not sufficient to maintain them with her child, he took a resolution of going from London, to try for a country school, which he thought himself well qualified to undertake, as he wrote an excellent hand, and was a master of arithmetic and accounts. This, however, he deemed a business below him, and confident of future better fortune, when he should be unwilling to have it known that he once was so meanly employed, he changed his name, and did me the honor to assume mine ; for I soon after had a letter from him, acquainting me that he was settled in a small village (in Berkshire, I think it was, where he taught reading and writing to ten or a dozen boys, at sixpence each per week), recommending Mrs. T—— to my care, and desiring me to write to him, directing for Mr. Franklin, schoolmaster, at such a place.

He continued to write frequently, sending me large specimens of an epic poem which he was then composing, and desiring my remarks and corrections. These I gave him from time to time, but endeavor'd rather to discourage his proceeding. One of Young's Satires was then just published. I copy'd and sent him a great part of it, which set in a strong light the folly of pursuing the Muses with any hope of advancement by them. All was in vain ; sheets of the poem continued to come by every post. In the meantime Mrs. T——, having on his account lost her friends and business, was often in distresses, and us'd to send for me, and borrow what I could spare to help her out of them. I grew fond of her company, and, being at that time under no religious restraint, and presuming upon my importance to her, I attempted familiarities (another erratum), which she repuls'd with a proper resentment, and acquainted him with my behaviour. This made a breach between us ; and, when he returned again to London, he let me know he thought I had cancell'd all the obligations he had been under to me. So I found I was never to expect his repaying me what I lent to him, or advanc'd for him. This, however, was not then of much consequence, as he was totally unable ; and in the loss of his friendship I found myself relieved from a burthen. I now began to think of getting a little money beforehand, and, expecting better work, I left Palmer's to work at Watts's, near Lincoln's Inn Fields, a still greater printing-house. Here I continued all the rest of my stay in London.

At my first admission into this printing-house I took to working at press, imagining I felt a want of the bodily exercise I had been us'd to in America, where presswork is mix'd with composing. I drank only water ; the other workmen, near fifty in number, were great guzzlers of beer. On occasion, I carried up and down stairs a large form of types in each hand, when others carried but one in both hands. They wondered to see, from this and several instances, that the *Water-American*, as they called me, was *stronger* than themselves, who drank *strong* beer ! We had an alehouse boy who attended always in the house to supply the workmen. My companion at the press drank every day a pint before breakfast, a pint at breakfast with his bread and cheese, a pint between breakfast and dinner, a pint at dinner, a pint in the afternoon about six o'clock, and another when he had done his day's work. I thought it a detestable custom ; but it was necessary, he suppos'd, to drink *strong* beer that he might be *strong* to labor. I endeavored to convince him that the bodily strength afforded by beer could only be in proportion to the grain or flour of the barley dissolved in the water of which it was made ; that there was more flour in a pennyworth of bread ; and therefore, if he would eat that with a pint of water, it would give him more strength than a quart of beer. He drank on, however, and had four or five shillings to pay out of his wages every Saturday night for that muddling liquor ; an expense I was free from. And thus these poor devils keep themselves always under.

Watts, after some weeks, desiring to have me in the composing-room, I left the press-men ; a new bien venu or sum for drink, being five shillings, was demanded of me by the compositors. I thought it an imposition, as I had paid below ; the master thought so too, and forbad my paying it. I stood out two or three weeks, was accordingly considered as an excommunicate, and had so many little pieces of private mischief done me, by mixing my sorts, transposing my pages, breaking my matter, etc., etc., if I were ever so little out of the room, and all ascribed to the chapel ghost, which they said ever haunted those not regularly admitted, that, notwithstanding the master's protection, I found myself oblig'd to comply and pay the money, convinc'd of the folly of being on ill terms with those one is to live with continually.

I was now on a fair footing with them, and soon acquir'd considerable influence. I propos'd some reasonable alterations in their chapel laws, and carried them against all opposition. From my example, a great part of them left their muddling breakfast of beer, and bread, and cheese, finding they could with me be supply'd from a neighboring house with a large porringer of hot water-gruel, sprinkled with pepper, crumb'd with bread, and a bit of butter in it, for the price of a pint of beer, viz., three half-pence. This was a more comfortable as well as cheaper breakfast, and kept their heads clearer. Those who continued sotting with beer all day, were often, by not paying, out of credit at the alehouse, and us'd to make interest with me to get beer ; their *light*, as they phrased it, *being out*. I watch'd the pay-table on Saturday night, and collected what I stood engag'd for them, having to pay sometimes near thirty shillings a week on their accounts. This, and my being esteem'd a pretty good *riggite*, that is, a jocular verbal satirist, supported my consequence in the society. My constant attendance (I never making a St. Monday) recommended me to the master ; and my uncommon quickness at composing occasioned my being put upon all work of dispatch, which was generally better paid. So I went on now very agreeably.

My lodging in Little Britain being too remote, I found another in Duke-street, opposite to the Romish Chapel. It was two pair of stairs backwards, at an Italian warehouse. A widow lady kept the house ; she had a daughter, and a maid servant, and a journeyman who attended the warehouse, but lodg'd abroad.   After sending to inquire my character at the house where I last lodg'd she agreed to take me in at the same rate, 3s. 6d. per week ; cheaper, as she said, from the protection she expected in having a man lodge in the house.   She was a widow, an elderly woman ; had been bred a Protestant, being a clergyman's daughter, but was converted to the Catholic religion by her husband, whose memory she much revered ; had lived much among people of distinction, and knew a thousand anecdotes of them as far back as the time of Charles the Second.   She was lame in her knees with the gout, and, therefore, seldom stirred out of her room, so sometimes wanted company ; and hers was so highly amusing to me, that I was sure to spend an evening with her whenever she desired it.   Our supper was only half an anchovy each, 'on a very little strip of bread and butter, and half a pint of ale between us ; but the entertainment was in her conversation.   My always keeping good hours, and giving little trouble in the family, made her unwilling to part with me ; so that, when I talk'd of a lodging I had heard of, nearer my business, for two shillings a week, which, intent as I now was on saving money, made some difference, she bid me not think of it, for she would abate me two shillings a week for the future ; so I remained with her at one shilling and sixpence as long as I staid in London.

In a garret of her house there lived a maiden lady of seventy, in the most retired manner, of whom my landlady gave me this account : that she was a Roman Catholic, had been sent abroad when young, and lodg'd in a nunnery with an intent of becoming a nun ; but, the country not agreeing with her, she returned to England, where, there being no nunnery, she had vow'd to lead the life of a nun, as near as might be done in those circumstances. Accordingly, she had given all her estate to charitable uses, reserving only twelve pounds a year to live on, and out of this sum she still gave a great deal in charity, living herself on water-gruel only, and using no fire but to boil it. She had lived many years in that garret, being permitted to remain there gratis by successive Catholic tenants of the house below, as they deemed it a blessing to have her there. A priest visited her to confess her every day. " I have ask'd her," says my landlady, " how she, as she liv'd, could possibly find so much employment for a confessor." " Oh," said she, " it is impossible to avoid *vain thoughts*." I was permitted once to visit her. She was cheerful and polite, and convers'd pleasantly. The room was clean, but had no other furniture than a matras, a table with a crucifix and book, a stool which she gave me to sit on, and a picture over the chimney of Saint Veronica displaying her handkerchief, with the miraculous figure of Christ's bleeding face on it, which she explained to me with great seriousness. She look'd pale, but was never sick ; and I give it as another instance on how small an income, life and health may be supported.

At Watts's printing-house I contracted an acquaintance with an ingenious young man, one Wygate, who, having wealthy relations, had been better educated than most printers ; was a tolerable Latinist, spoke French, and lov'd reading. I taught him and a friend of his to swim at twice going into the river, and they soon became good swimmers. They introduc'd me to some gentlemen from the country, who went to Chelsea by water to see the College and Don Saltero's curiosities. In our return, at the request of the company, whose curiosity Wygate had excited, I stripped and leaped into the river, and swam from near Chelsea to Blackfriar's, performing on the way many feats of activity, both upon and under the water, that surpris'd and pleas'd those to whom they were novelties.

I had from a child been ever delighted with this exercise, had studied and practis'd all Thevenot's motions and positions, added some of my own, aiming at the graceful and easy as well as the useful. All these I took this occasion of exhibiting to the company, and was much flatter'd by their admiration ; and Wygate, who was desirous of becoming a master, grew more and more attach'd to me on that account, as well as from the similarity of our studies. He at length proposed to me travelling all over Europe together, supporting ourselves everywhere by working at our business. I was once inclined to it; but, mentioning it to my good friend, Mr. Denham, with whom I often spent an hour when I had leisure, he dissuaded me from it, advising me to think only of returning to Pennsylvania, which he was now about to do.

I must record one trait of this good man's character. He had formerly been in business at Bristol, but failed in debt to a number of people, compounded and went to America. There, by a close application to business as a merchant, he acquir'd a plentiful fortune in a few years. Returning to England in the ship with me, he invited his old creditors to an entertainment, at which he thank'd them for the easy composition they had favored him with, and, when they expected nothing but the treat, every man at the first remove found under his plate an order on a banker for the full amount of the unpaid remainder, with interest.

He now told me he was about to return to Philadelphia, and should carry over a great quantity of goods, in order to open a store there. He propos'd to take me over as his clerk, to keep his books, in which he would instruct me, copy his letters, and attend the store. He added, that, as soon as I should be acquainted with mercantile business, he would promote me by sending me with a cargo of flour and bread, etc., to the West Indies, and procure me commissions from others which would be profitable ; and, if I manag'd well, would establish me handsomely. The thing pleas'd me ; for I was grown tired of London, remembered with pleasure the happy months I had spent in Pennsylvania, and wish'd again to see it ; therefore I immediately agreed on the terms of fifty pounds a year, Pennsylvania money ; less, indeed, than my present gettings as a compositor, but affording a better prospect.

I now took leave of printing, as I thought, for ever, and was daily employ'd in my new business, going about with Mr. Denham among the tradesmen to purchase various articles, and seeing them pack'd up, doing errands, calling upon workmen to dispatch, etc.; and, when all was on board, I had a few days' leisure. On one of these days, I was, to my surprise, sent for by a great man I knew only by name, a Sir William Wyndham, and I waited upon him. He had heard by some means or other of my swimming from Chelsea to Blackfriar's, and of my teaching Wygate and another young man to swim in a few hours.. He had two sons, about to set out on their travels ; he wish'd to have them first taught swimming, and proposed to gratify me handsomely if I would teach them. They were not yet come to town, and my stay was uncertain, so I could not undertake it ; but from this incident I thought it

Early Life

likely that, if I were to remain in England and open a swimming-school, I might get a good deal of money ; and it struck me so strongly, that, had the overture been sooner made me, probably I should not so soon have returned to America. After many years, you and I had something of more importance to do with one of these sons of Sir William Wyndham, become Earl of Egremont, which I shall mention in its place.

Thus I spent about eighteen months in London ; most part of the time I work'd hard at my business, and spent but little upon myself except in seeing plays and in books. My friend Ralph had kept me poor ; he owed me about twenty-seven pounds, which I was now never likely to receive ; a great sum out of my small earnings ! I lov'd him, notwithstanding, for he had many amiable qualities. I had by no means improv'd my fortune ; but I had picked up some very ingenious acquaintance, whose conversation was of great advantage to me ; and I had read considerably.

We sail'd from Gravesend on the 23d of July, 1726. For the incidents of the voyage, I refer you to my Journal, where you will find them all minutely related. Perhaps the most important part of that journal is the *plan* to be found in it, which I formed at sea, for regulating my future conduct in life. It is the more remarkable, as being formed when I was so young, and yet being pretty faithfully adhered to quite thro' old age.

Settling Down.

A friendly correspondence as neighbors and old acquaintances had continued between me and Mr. Read's family, who all had a regard for me from the time of my first lodging in their house. I was often invited there and consulted in their affairs, wherein I sometimes was of service. I piti'd poor Miss Read's* unfortunate situation, who was generally dejected, seldom cheerful, and avoided company. I considered my giddiness and inconstancy when in London as in a great degree the cause of her unhappiness, tho' the mother was good enough to think the fault more her own than mine, as she had prevented our marrying before I went thither, and persuaded the other match in my absence. Our mutual affection was revived, but there were now great objections to our union. The match was indeed looked upon as invalid, a preceding wife being said to be living in England; but this could not easily be prov'd, because of the distance; and, tho' there was a report of his death, it was not certain. Then, tho' it should be true, he had left many debts,

* She had in the interval made an unhappy marriage, and was separated from her husband.

Settling Down

which his successor might be call'd upon to pay. We ventured, however, over all these difficulties, and I took her to wife, September 1st, 1730. None of the inconveniences happened that we had apprehended ; she proved a good and faithful helpmate, assisted me much by attending shop ; we throve together, and have ever mutually endeavor'd to make each other happy. Thus I corrected that great *erratum* as well as I could.*

About this time, our club meeting, not at a tavern, but in a little room of Mr. Grace's, set apart for that purpose, a proposition was made by me, that, since our books were often referr'd to in our disquisitions upon the queries, it might be convenient to us to have them altogether where we met, that upon occasion they might be consulted ; and by thus clubbing our books to a common library, we should, while we lik'd to keep them together, have each of us the advantage of using the books of all the other members, which would be nearly as beneficial as if each owned the whole. It was lik'd and agreed to, and we fill'd one end of the room with such books as we could best spare. The number was not so great as we expected ; and tho' they had been of great use, yet some inconveniences occurring for want of due care of them, the collection, after about a year, was separated, and each took his books home again.

* Mrs. Franklin survived her marriage over forty years. She died December 19, 1774.—ED.

Benjamin Franklin

And now I set on foot my first project of a
public nature, that for a subscription library.
I drew up the proposals, got them put into form
by our great scrivener, Brockden, and, by the
help of my friends in the Junto,* procured fifty
subscribers of forty shillings each to begin with,
and ten shillings a year for fifty years, the term
our company was to continue. We afterwards
obtain'd a charter, the company being increased
to one hundred ; this was the mother of all the
North American subscription libraries, now so
numerous. It is become a great thing itself,
and continually increasing. These libraries
have improved the general conversation of the
Americans, made the common tradesmen and
farmers as intelligent as most gentlemen from
other countries, and perhaps have contributed
in some degree to the stand so generally made
throughout the colonies in defence of their
privileges.

At the time I establish'd myself in Pennsylvania, there was not a good bookseller's shop in
any of the colonies to the southward of Boston.
In New York and Philadelphia the printers
were indeed stationers ; they sold only paper,
etc., almanacs, ballads, and a few common
school-books. Those who lov'd reading were
oblig'd to send for their books from England ;
the members of the Junto had each a few. We

* A young men's club for mutual improvement,
formed by Franklin.

had left the alehouse, where we first met, and hired a room to hold our club in. I propos'd that we should all of us bring our books to that room, where they would not only be ready to consult in our conferences, but become a common benefit, each of us being at liberty to borrow such as he wish'd to read at home. This was accordingly done, and for some time contented us.

Finding the advantage of this little collection, I propos'd to render the benefit from books more common, by commencing a public subscription library. I drew a sketch of the plan and rules that would be necessary, and got a skilful conveyancer, Mr. Charles Brockden, to put the whole in form of articles of agreement to be subscribed, by which each subscriber engag'd to pay a certain sum down for the first purchase of books, and an annual contribution for increasing them. So few were the readers at that time in Philadelphia, and the majority of us so poor, that I was not able, with great industry, to find more than fifty persons, mostly young tradesmen, willing to pay down for this purpose forty shillings each, and ten shillings per annum. On this little fund we began. The books were imported ; the library was opened one day in the week for lending to the subscribers, on their promissory notes to pay double the value if not duly returned. The institution soon manifested its utility, was imitated by other towns, and in other provinces.

Benjamin Franklin

The libraries were augmented by donations ; reading became fashionable ; and our people, having no public amusements to divert their attention from study, became better acquainted with books, and in a few years were observ'd by strangers to be better instructed and more intelligent than people of the same rank generally are in other countries.

When we were about to sign the above-mentioned articles, which were to be binding on us, our heirs, etc., for fifty years, Mr. Brockden, the scrivener, said to us : "You are young men, but it is scarcely probable that any of you will live to see the expiration of the term fix'd in the instrument." A number of us, however, are yet living ; but the instrument was after a few years rendered null by a charter that incorporated and gave perpetuity to the company.

The objections and reluctances I met with in soliciting the subscriptions, made me soon feel the impropriety of presenting one's self as the proposer of any useful project, that might be suppos'd to raise one's reputation in the smallest degree above that of one's neighbors, when one has need of their assistance to accomplish that project. I therefore put myself as much as I could out of sight, and stated it as a scheme of a *number of friends*, who had requested me to go about and propose it to such as they thought lovers of reading. In this way my affair went on more smoothly, and I ever after practis'd it on such occasions ; and, from my

Settling Down

frequent successes, can heartily recommend it. The present little sacrifice of your vanity will afterwards be amply repaid. If it remains a while uncertain to whom the merit belongs, some one more vain than yourself will be encouraged to claim it, and then even envy will be disposed to do you justice by plucking those assumed feathers, and restoring them to their right owner.

This library afforded me the means of improvement by constant study, for which I set apart an hour or two each day, and thus repair'd in some degree the loss of the learned education my father once intended for me. Reading was the only amusement I allow'd myself. I spent no time in taverns, games, or frolics of any kind ; and my industry in my business continu'd as indefatigable as it was necessary. I was indebted for my printing-house ; I had a young family coming on to be educated, and I had to contend with for business two printers, who were established in the place before me. My circumstances, however, grew daily easier. My original habits of frugality continuing, and my father having, among his instructions to me when a boy, frequently repeated a proverb of Solomon, " Seest thou a man diligent in his calling, he shall stand before kings, he shall not stand before mean men," I from thence considered industry as a means of obtaining wealth and distinction, which encourag'd me, tho' I did not think that

Benjamin Franklin

I should ever literally *stand before kings*, which, however, has since happened ; for I have stood before *five*, and even had the honor of sitting down with one, the King of Denmark, to dinner.

We have an English proverb that says, "*He that would thrive, must ask his wife.*" It was lucky for me that I had one as much dispos'd to industry and frugality as myself. She assisted me cheerfully in my business, folding and stitching pamphlets, tending shop, purchasing old linen rags for the paper-makers, etc., etc. We kept no idle servants, our table was plain and simple, our furniture of the cheapest. For instance, my breakfast was a long time bread and milk (no tea), and I ate it out of a twopenny earthen porringer, with a pewter spoon. But mark how luxury will enter families, and make a progress, in spite of principle : being call'd one morning to breakfast, I found it in a china bowl, with a spoon of silver ! They had been bought for me without my knowledge by my wife, and had cost her the enormous sum of three-and-twenty shillings, for which she had no other excuse or apology to make, but that she thought *her* husband deserv'd a silver spoon and china bowl as well as any of his neighbors. This was the first appearance of plate and china in our house, which afterward, in a course of years, as our wealth increas'd, augmented gradually to several hundred pounds in value.

Settling Down

I had been religiously educated as a Presbyterian ; and tho' some of the dogmas of that persuasion, such as *the eternal decrees of God, election, reprobation, etc.*, appeared to me unintelligible, others doubtful, and I early absented myself from the public assemblies of the sect, Sunday being my studying day, I never was without some religious principles. I never doubted, for instance, the existence of the Deity ; that he made the world, and govern'd it by his Providence ; that the most acceptable service of God was the doing good to man ; that our souls are immortal ; and that all crime will be punished, and virtue rewarded, either here or hereafter. These I esteem'd the essentials of every religion ; and, being to be found in all the religions we had in our country, I respected them all, tho' with different degrees of respect, as I found them more or less mix'd with other articles, which, without any tendency to inspire, promote, or confirm morality, serv'd principally to divide us, and make us unfriendly to one another. This respect to all, with an opinion that the worst had some good effects, induc'd me to avoid all discourse that might tend to lessen the good opinion another might have of his own religion ; and as our province increas'd in people, and new places of worship were continually wanted, and generally erected by voluntary contribution, my mite for such purpose, whatever might be the sect, was never refused.

Benjamin Franklin

Tho' I seldom attended any public worship, I had still an opinion of its propriety, and of its utility when rightly conducted, and I regularly paid my annual subscription for the support of the only Presbyterian minister or meeting we had in Philadelphia. He us'd to visit me sometimes as a friend, and admonish me to attend his administrations, and I was now and then prevail'd on to do so, once for five Sundays successively. Had he been in my opinion a good preacher, perhaps I might have continued, notwithstanding the occasion I had for the Sunday's leisure in my course of study ; but his discourses were chiefly either polemic arguments, or explications of the peculiar doctrines of our sect, and were all to me very dry, uninteresting, and unedifying, since not a single moral principle was inculcated or enforc'd, their aim seeming to be rather to make us Presbyterians than good citizens.

At length he took for his text that verse of the fourth chapter of Philippians : " *Finally, brethren, whatsoever things are true, honest, just, pure, lovely, or of good report, if there be any virtue, or any praise, think on these things.*" And I imagin'd, in a sermon on such a text, we could not miss of having some morality. But he confin'd himself to five points only, as meant by the apostle, viz.: 1. Keeping holy the Sabbath day. 2. Being diligent in reading the holy Scriptures. 3. Attending duly the public worship. 4. Partaking of the Sac-

Settling Down

rament. 5. Paying a due respect to God's ministers. These might be all good things ; but, as they were not the kind of good things that I expected from that text, I despaired of ever meeting with them from any other, was disgusted, and attended his preaching no more. I had some years before compos'd a little Liturgy, or form of prayer, for my own private use (viz., in 1728), entitled " Articles of Belief and Acts of Religion." I return'd to the use of this, and went no more to the public assemblies. My conduct might be blamable, but I leave it, without attempting further to excuse it ; my present purpose being to relate facts, and not to make apologies for them.

Rules of Conduct.

It was about this time I conceiv'd the bold and arduous project of arriving at moral perfection. I wish'd to live without committing any fault at any time ; I would conquer all that either natural inclination, custom, or company might lead me into. As I knew, or thought I knew, what was right and wrong, I did not see why I might not always do the one and avoid the other. But I soon found I had undertaken a task of more difficulty than I had imagined. While my care was employ'd in guarding against one fault, I was often surprised by another ; habit took the advantage of inattention ; inclination was sometimes too strong for reason. I concluded, at length, that the mere speculative conviction that it was our interest to be completely virtuous, was not sufficient to prevent our slipping ; and that the contrary habits must be broken, and good ones acquired and established, before we can have any dependence on a steady, uniform rectitude of conduct. For this purpose I therefore contrived the following method.

In the various enumerations of the moral virtues I had met with in my reading, I found the

66

Rules of Conduct

catalogue more or less numerous, as different writers included more or fewer ideas under the same name. Temperance, for example, was by some confined to eating and drinking, while by others it was extended to mean the moderating every other pleasure, appetite, inclination, or passion, bodily or mental, even to our avarice and ambition. I propos'd to myself, for the sake of clearness, to use rather more names, with fewer ideas annex'd to each, than a few names with more ideas ; and I included under thirteen names of virtues all that at that time occurr'd to me as necessary or desirable, and annexed to each a short precept, which fully express'd the extent I gave to its meaning.

These names of virtues, with their precepts, were :

1. TEMPERANCE.

Eat not to dullness ; drink not to elevation.

2. SILENCE.

Speak not but what may benefit others or yourself ; avoid trifling conversation.

3. ORDER.

Let all your things have their places ; let each part of your business have its time.

4. RESOLUTION.

Resolve to perform what you ought ; perform without fail what you resolve.

5. FRUGALITY.

Make no expense but to do good to others or yourself ; *i.e.*, waste nothing.

6. INDUSTRY.

Lose no time ; be always employ'd in something useful ; cut off all unnecessary actions.

7. SINCERITY.

Use no hurtful deceit ; think innocently and justly ; and, if you speak, speak accordingly.

8. JUSTICE.

Wrong none by doing injuries, or omitting the benefits that are your duty.

9. MODERATION.

Avoid extremes ; forbear resenting injuries so much as you think they deserve.

10. CLEANLINESS.

Tolerate no uncleanliness in body, clothes, or habitation.

11. TRANQUILLITY.

Be not disturbed at trifles, or at accidents common or unavoidable.

12. CHASTITY.

Rarely use venery but for health or offspring, never to dullness, weakness, or the injury of your own or another's peace or reputation.

Rules of Conduct

13. HUMILITY.

Imitate Jesus and Socrates.

My intention being to acquire the *habitude* of all these virtues, I judg'd it would be well not to distract my attention by attempting the whole at once, but to fix it on one of them at a time ; and, when I should be master of that, then to proceed to another, and so on, till I should have gone through the thirteen ; and, as the previous acquisition of some might facilitate the acquisition of certain others, I arrang'd them with that view, as they stand above. Temperance first, as it tends to procure that coolness and clearness of head, which is so necessary where constant vigilance was to be kept up, and guard maintained against the unremitting attraction of ancient habits, and the force of perpetual temptations. This being acquir'd and establish'd, Silence would be more easy ; and my desire being to gain knowledge at the same time that I improv'd in virtue, and considering that in conversation it was obtain'd rather by the use of the ears than of the tongue, and therefore wishing to break a habit I was getting into of prattling, punning, and joking, which only made me acceptable to trifling company, I gave *Silence* the second place. This and the next, *Order*, I expected would allow me more time for attending to my project and my studies. *Resolution*, once become habitual, would keep me firm in my endeavors to obtain all the subsequent virtues ; *Frugality* and

89

Benjamin Franklin

Industry, freeing me from my remaining debt, and producing affluence and independence, would make more easy the practice of *Sincerity* and *Justice*, etc., etc. Conceiving then, that, agreeably to the advice of Pythagoras in his Golden Verses, daily examination would be necessary, I contrived the following method for conducting that examination.

I made a little book, in which I allotted a page for each of the virtues. I rul'd each page with red ink, so as to have seven columns, one for each day of the week, marking each column with a letter for the day. I cross'd these columns with thirteen red lines, marking the beginning of each line with the first letter of one of the virtues, on which line, and in its proper column, I might mark, by a little black spot, every fault I found upon examination to have been committed respecting that virtue upon that day.

I determined to give a week's strict attention to each of the virtues successively. Thus, in the first week, my great guard was to avoid every the least offence agaist *Temperance*, leaving the other virtues to their ordinary chance, only marking every evening the faults of the day. Thus, if in the first week I could keep my first line, marked T, clear of spots, I suppos'd the habit of that virtue so much strengthen'd, and its opposite weaken'd, that I might venture extending my attention to include the next, and for the following week keep both lines clear of

Rules of Conduct

Form of the Pages.

TEMPERANCE.						
EAT NOT TO DULNESS ; DRINK NOT TO ELEVATION.						
	S.	M.	T.	W.	T.	F.	S.
T.							
S.	*	*		*		*	
O.	**	*	*		*	*	*
R.			*			*	
F.		*			*		
I.			*				
S.							
J.							
M.							
C.							
T.							
C.							
H.							

spots. Proceeding thus to the last, I could go thro' a course complete in thirteen weeks, and four courses in a year. And like him who, having a garden to weed, does not attempt to eradicate all the bad herbs at once, which would exceed his reach and his strength, but works

on one of the beds at a time, and, having accomplish'd the first, proceeds to a second, so I
should have, I hoped, the encouraging pleasure
of seeing on my pages the progress I made in
virtue, by clearing successively my lines of
their spots, till in the end, by a number of
courses, I should be happy in viewing a clean
book, after a thirteen weeks' daily examination.

This my little book had for its motto these
lines from Addison's *Cato* :

"Here will I hold. If ther 's a power above us
(And that there is, all nature cries aloud
Thro' all her works), He must delight in virtue ;
And that which he delights in must be happy."

Another from Cicero :

"O vitæ Philosophia dux ! O virtutum indagatrix
expultrixque vitiorum! Unus dies, bene et ex præceptis
tuis actus, peccanti immortalitati est anteponendus."

Another from the Proverbs of Solomon,
speaking of wisdom or virtue :

"Length of days is in her right hand, and in her left
hand riches and honor. Her ways are ways of pleas-
antness, and all her paths are peace." iii. 16, 17.

And conceiving God to be the fountain of
wisdom, I thought it right and necessary to
solicit his assistance for obtaining it ; to this
end I formed the following little prayer, which
was prefix'd to my tables of examination, for
daily use :

"*O powerful Goodness ! bountiful Father ! merciful
Guide ! Increase in me that wisdom which discovers my
truest interest. Strengthen my resolutions to perform
what that wisdom dictates. Accept my kind offices to*

Rules of Conduct

thy other children as the only return in my power for thy continual favours to me.

I used also sometimes a little prayer which I took from Thomson's Poems, viz.:

"Father of light and life, thou Good Supreme!
O teach me what is good; teach me Thyself!
Save me from folly, vanity, and vice,
From every low pursuit; and fill my soul
With knowledge, conscious peace, and virtue pure;
Sacred, substantial, never-fading bliss!"

The precept of *Order* requiring that *every part of my business should have its allotted time*, one page in my little book contain'd the following scheme of employment for the twenty-four hours of a natural day.

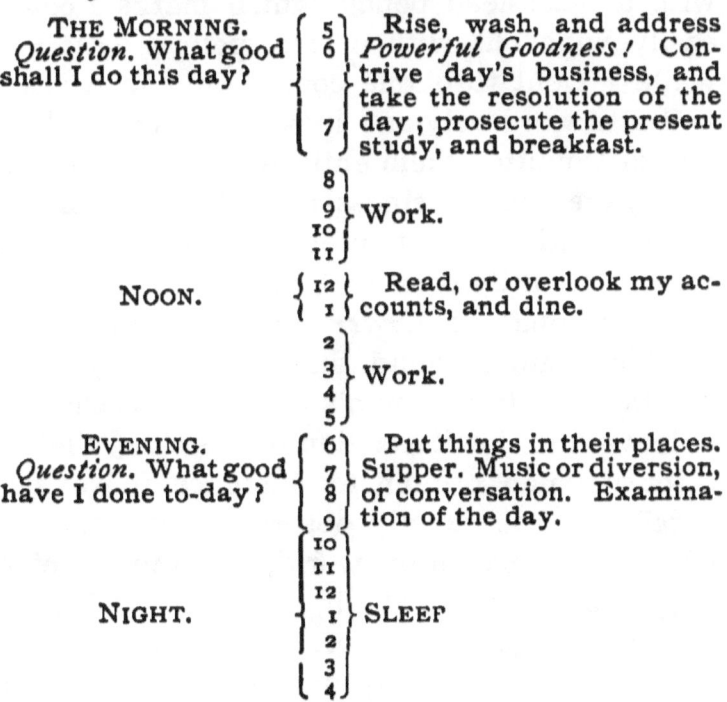

THE MORNING. *Question.* What good shall I do this day?	5 6 7	Rise, wash, and address *Powerful Goodness!* Contrive day's business, and take the resolution of the day; prosecute the present study, and breakfast.
	8 9 10 11	Work.
NOON.	12 1	Read, or overlook my accounts, and dine.
	2 3 4 5	Work.
EVENING. *Question.* What good have I done to-day?	6 7 8 9	Put things in their places. Supper. Music or diversion, or conversation. Examination of the day.
NIGHT.	10 11 12 1 2 3 4	SLEEP

93

Benjamin Franklin

I enter'd upon the execution of this plan for self-examination, and continu'd it with occasional intermissions for some time. I was surpris'd to find myself so much fuller of faults than I had imagined; but I had the satisfaction of seeing them diminish. To avoid the trouble of renewing now and then my little book, which, by scraping out the marks on the paper of old faults to make room for new ones in a new course, became full of holes, I transferr'd my tables and precepts to the ivory leaves of a memorandum book, on which the lines were drawn with red ink, that made a durable stain, and on those lines I mark'd my faults with a black-lead pencil, which marks I could easily wipe out with a wet sponge. After a while I went thro' one course only in a year, and afterward only one in several years, till at length I omitted them entirely, being employ'd in voyages and business abroad, with a multiplicity of affairs that interfered; but I always carried my little book with me.

My scheme of *Order* gave me the most trouble; and I found that, tho' it might be practicable where a man's business was such as to leave him the disposition of his time, that of a journeyman printer, for instance, it was not possible to be exactly observed by a master, who must mix with the world, and often receive people of business at their own hours. *Order*, too, with regard to places for things, papers, etc., I found extremely difficult to acquire. I

Rules of Conduct

had not been early accustomed to it, and, having an exceeding good memory, I was not so sensible of the inconvenience attending want of method. This article, therefore, cost me so much painful attention, and my faults in it vexed me so much, and I made so little progress in amendment, and had such frequent relapses, that I was almost ready to give up the attempt, and content myself with a faulty character in that respect, like the man who, in buying an ax of a smith, my neighbor, desired to have the whole of its surface as bright as the edge. The smith consented to grind it bright for him if he would turn the wheel ; he turn'd, while the smith press'd the broad face of the ax hard and heavily on the stone, which made the turning of it very fatiguing. The man came every now and then from the wheel to see how the work went on, and at length would take his ax as it was, without farther grinding. " No," said the smith, " turn on, turn on ; we shall have it bright by-and-by ; as yet, it is only speckled." " Yes," says the man, " *but I think I like a speckled ax best.*" And I believe this may have been the case with many, who, having, for want of some such means as I employ'd, found the difficulty of obtaining good and breaking bad habits in other points of vice and virtue, have given up the struggle, and concluded that " *a speckled ax was best*" ; For something, that pretended to be reason, was every now and then suggesting to me that such extreme nicety as I exacted of myself might be a kind of foppery in morals, which, if it were known, would make me ridiculous ; that a perfect character might be attended with the inconvenience of being envied and hated ; and that a benevolent man should allow a few faults in himself, to keep his friends in countenance.

In truth, I found myself incorrigible with respect to *order ;* and now I am grown old, and my memory bad, I feel very sensibly the want ōf it. But, on the whole, tho' I never arrived at the perfection I had been so ambitious of obtaining, but fell far short of it, yet I was, by the endeavour, a better and a happier man than I otherwise should have been if I had not attempted it ; as those who aim at perfect writing by imitating the engraved copies, tho' they never reach the wish'd-for excellence of those copies, their hand is mended by the endeavour, and is tolerable while it continues fair and legible.

It may be well my posterity should be informed that to this little artifice, with the blessing of God, their ancestor ow'd the constant felicity of his life, down to his 79th year, in which this is written. What reverses may attend the remainder is in the hand of Providence ; but, if they arrive, the reflection on past happiness enjoy'd ought to help his bearing them with more resignation. To Temperance he ascribes his long-continued health, and what is still left to him of a good constitution ; to Industry and Frugality, the early easiness of his circumstances and acquisition of his fortune, with all that knowledge that enabled him to be a useful citizen, and obtained for him some degree of reputation among the learned ; to Sincerity and Justice, the confidence of his country, and the honorable employs it conferred upon him ; and to the joint influence of the whole mass of the virtues, even in the imperfect state he was able to acquire them, all that evenness of temper, and that cheerfulness in conversation, which makes his company still sought for, and agreeable even to his younger acquaintance. I hope, therefore, that some of my descendants may follow the example and reap the benefit.

It will be remark'd that, tho' my scheme was not wholly without religion, there was in it no mark of any of the distinguishing tenets of any particular sect. I had purposely avoided them ; for, being fully persuaded of the utility and excellency of my method, and that it might be serviceable to people in all religions, and intending some time or other to publish it, I would not have any thing in it that should prejudice any one, of any sect, against it. I purposed writing a little comment on each virtue, in which I would have shown the advantages of possessing it, and the mischiefs attending its opposite vice ; and I should have called my book " The Art of Virtue,"* because it would

---

* Nothing so likely to make a man's fortune as virtue.
—[Marg. note.]

have shown the means and manner of obtaining virtue, which would have distinguished it from the mere exhortation to be good, that does not instruct and indicate the means, but is like the apostle's man of verbal charity, who only without showing to the naked and hungry how or where they might get clothes or victuals, exhorted them to be fed and clothed.—James ii. 15, 16.

But it so happened that my intention of writing and publishing this comment was never fulfilled. I did, indeed, from time to time, put down short hints of the sentiments, reasonings, etc., to be made use of in it, some of which I have still by me ; but the necessary close attention to private business in the earlier part of my life, and public business since, have occasioned my postponing it ; for, it being connected in my mind with *a great and extensive project*, that required the whole man to execute, and which an unforeseen succession of employs prevented my attending to, it has hitherto remain'd unfinish'd.

In this piece it was my design to explain and enforce this doctrine, that vicious actions are not hurtful because they are forbidden, but forbidden because they are hurtful, the nature of man alone considered ; that it was, therefore, every one's interest to be virtuous who wish'd to be happy even in this world ; and I should, from this circumstance (there being always in the world a number of rich merchants, nobility,

Rules of Conduct

states, and princes, who have need of honest
instruments for the management of their affairs,
and such being so rare), have endeavored to
convince young persons that no qualities were
so likely to make a poor man's fortune as those
of probity and integrity.

My list of virtues contain'd at first but twelve ;
but a Quaker friend having kindly informed
me that I was generally thought proud ; that
my pride show'd itself frequently in conversation ; that I was not content with being in the
right when discussing any point, but was over-
bearing, and rather insolent, of which he convinc'd me by mentioning several instances ; I
determined endeavouring to cure myself, if I
could, of this vice or folly among the rest, and
I added *Humility* to my list, giving an extensive meaning to the word.

I cannot boast of much success in acquiring
the *reality* of this virtue, but I had a good deal
with regard to the *appearance* of it. I made
it a rule to forbear all direct contradiction to
the sentiments of others, and all positive asser-
tion of my own. I even forbid myself, agreeably to the old laws of our Junto, the use of
every word or expression in the language that
imported a fix'd opinion, such as *certainly, undoubtedly*, etc., and I adopted, instead of them,
I conceive, I apprehend, or *I imagine* a thing
to be so or so ; or it *so appears to me at present.* When another asserted something that I
thought an error, I deny'd myself the pleasure

of contradicting him abruptly, and of showing immediately some absurdity in his proposition; and in answering I began by observing that in certain cases or circumstances his opinion would be right, but in the present case there *appear'd* or *seem'd* to me some difference, etc. I soon found the advantage of this change in my manner; the conversations I engag'd in went on more pleasantly. The modest way in which I propos'd my opinions procur'd them a readier reception and less contradiction; I had less mortification when I was found to be in the wrong, and I more easily prevail'd with others to give up their mistakes and join with me when I happened to be in the right.

And this mode, which I at first put on with some violence to natural inclination, became at length so easy, and so habitual to me, that perhaps for these fifty years past no one has ever heard a dogmatical expression escape me. And to this habit (after my character of integrity) I think it principally owing that I had early so much weight with my fellow-citizens when I proposed new institutions, or alterations in the old, and so much influence in public councils when I became a member; for I was but a bad speaker, never eloquent, subject to much hesitation in my choice of words, hardly correct in language, and yet I generally carried my points.

In reality, there is, perhaps, no one of our natural passions so hard to subdue as *pride*. Disguise it, struggle with it, beat it down, stifle

Rules of Conduct

it, mortify it as much as one pleases, it is still alive, and will every now and then peep out and show himself ; you will see it, perhaps, often in this history ; for, even if I could conceive that I had completely overcome it, I should probably be proud of my humility.

[Thus far written at Passy, 1784.]

Public Affairs.

My first promotion was my being chosen, in 1736, clerk of the General Assembly. The choice was made that year without opposition ; but the year following, when I was again pro- pos'd (the choice, like that of the members, being annual), a new member made a long speech against me, in order to favour some other candidate. I was, however, chosen, which was the more agreeable to me, as, be- sides the pay for the immediate service as clerk, the place gave me a better opportunity of keep- ing up an interest among the members, which secur'd to me the business of printing the votes, laws, paper money, and other occasional jobs for the public, that, on the whole, were very profitable.

I therefore did not like the opposition of this new member, who was a gentleman of fortune and education, with talents that were likely to give him, in time, great influence in the House, which, indeed, afterwards happened. I did not, however, aim at gaining his favour by pay- ing any servile respect to him, but, after some time, took this other method. Having heard that he had in his library a certain very scarce

and curious book, I wrote a note to him, expressing my desire of perusing that book, and
requesting he would do me the favour of lending it to me for a few days. He sent it immediately, and I return'd it in about a week with
another note, expressing strongly my sense of
the favour. When we next met in the House,
he spoke to me (which he had never done before), and with great civility ; and he ever after
manifested a readiness to serve me on all occasions, so that we became great friends, and our
friendship continued to his death. This is another instance of the truth of an old maxim I
had learned, which says : " *He that has once
done you a kindness will be more ready to do
you another, than he whom you yourself have
obliged.*" And it shows how much more profitable it is prudently to remove, than to resent,
return, and continue inimical proceedings.

In 1737, Colonel Spotswood, late governor of
Virginia, and then postmaster-general, being
dissatisfied with the conduct of his deputy at
Philadelphia, respecting some negligence in
rendering, and inexactitude of his accounts,
took from him the commission and offered it to
me. I accepted it readily, and found it of great
advantage ; for, tho' the salary was small, it
facilitated the correspondence that improv'd
my newspaper, increas'd the number demanded, as well as the advertisements to be inserted,
so that it came to afford me a considerable income. My old competitor's newspaper declin'd

proportionably, and I was satisfy'd without re-
taliating his refusal, while postmaster, to permit my papers being carried by the riders.
Thus he suffer'd greatly from his neglect in due
accounting ; and I mention it as a lesson to
those young men who may be employ'd in
managing affairs for others, that they should
always render accounts, and make remittances,
with great clearness and punctuality. The
character of observing such a conduct is the
most powerful of all recommendations to new
employments and increase of business.

I began now to turn my thoughts a little to
public affairs, beginning, however, with small
matters. The city watch was one of the first
things that I conceiv'd to want regulation. It
was managed by the constables of the respective wards in turn ; the constable warned a
number of housekeepers to attend him for the
night. Those who chose never to attend, paid
him six shillings a year to be excus'd, which
was suppos'd to be for hiring substitutes, but
was, in reality, much more than was necessary
for that purpose, and made the constableship a
place of profit ; and the constable, for a little
drink, often got such ragamuffins about him as
a watch, that respectable housekeepers did not
choose to mix with. Walking the rounds, too,
was often neglected, and most of the nights
spent in tippling. I thereupon wrote a paper
to be read in Junto, representing these irregu-
larities, but insisting more particularly on the

inequality of this six-shilling tax of the constables, respecting the circumstances of those who
paid it, since a poor widow housekeeper, all
whose property to be guarded by the watch did
not perhaps exceed the value of fifty pounds,
paid as much as the wealthiest merchant, who
had thousands of pounds' worth of goods in his
stores.

On the whole, I proposed as a more effectual
watch, the hiring of proper men to serve con-
stantly in that business ; and as a more equita-
ble way of supporting the charge, the levying
a tax that should be proportion'd to the property. This idea, being approv'd by the Junto,
was communicated to the other clubs, but as
arising in each of them ; and though the plan
was not immediately carried into execution,
yet, by preparing the minds of people for the
change, it paved the way for the law obtained
a few years after, when the members of our
clubs were grown into more influence.

About this time I wrote a paper (first to be
read in Junto, but it was afterward publish'd)
on the different accidents and carelessnesses
by which houses were set on fire, with cautions
against them, and means proposed of avoiding
them. This was much spoken of as a useful
piece, and gave rise to a project, which soon
followed it, of forming a company for the more
ready extinguishing of fires, and mutual assistance in removing and securing of goods when
in danger. Associates in this scheme were

presently found, amounting to thirty. Our
articles of agreement oblig'd every member to
keep always in good order, and fit for use, a
certain number of leather buckets, with strong
bags and baskets (for packing and transporting
of goods), which were to be brought to every
fire ; and we agreed to meet once a month and
spend a social evening together, in discoursing
and communicating such ideas as occurred to
us upon the subject of fires, as might be useful
in our conduct on such occasions.

The utility of this institution soon appeared,
and many more desiring to be admitted than
we thought convenient for one company, they
were advised to form another, which was accordingly done ; and this went on, one new
company being formed after another, till they
became so numerous as to include most of the
inhabitants who were men of property ; and
now, at the time of my writing this, tho' up-
ward of fifty years since its establishment, that
which I first formed, called the Union Fire
Company, still subsists and flourishes, tho' the
first members are all deceas'd but myself and
one, who is older by a year than I am. The
small fines that have been paid by members for
absence at the monthly meetings have been apply'd to the purchase of fire-engines, ladders,
fire-hooks, and other useful implements for each
company, so that I question whether there is a
city in the world better provided with the
means of putting a stop to beginning conflagra-

tions ; and, in fact, since these institutions, the city has never lost by fire more than one or two houses at a time, and the flames have often been extinguished before the house in which they began has been half consumed.

George Whitefield.

In 1739 arrived among us from Ireland the Reverend Mr. Whitefield, who had made himself remarkable there as an itinerant preacher. He was at first permitted to preach in some of our churches ; but the clergy, taking a dislike to him, soon refus'd him their pulpits, and he was oblig'd to preach in the fields. The multitudes of all sects and denominations that attended his sermons were enormous, and it was matter of speculation to me, who was one of the number, to observe the extraordinary influence of his oratory on his hearers, and how much they admir'd and respected him, notwithstanding his common abuse of them, by assuring them they were naturally *half beasts and half devils.* It was wonderful to see the change soon made in the manners of our inhabitants. From being thoughtless or indifferent about religion, it seem'd as if all the world were growing religious, so that one could not walk thro' the town in an evening without hearing psalms sung in different families of every street.

And it being found inconvenient to assemble in the open air, subject to its inclemencies, the building of a house to meet in was no sooner propos'd, and persons appointed to receive contributions, but sufficient sums were soon receiv'd to procure the ground and erect the building, which was one hundred feet long and seventy broad, about the size of Westminster Hall ; and the work was carried on with such spirit as to be finished in a much shorter time than could have been expected. Both house and ground were vested in trustees, expressly for the use of any preacher of any religious persuasion who might desire to say something to the people of Philadelphia ; the design in building not being to accommodate any particular sect, but the inhabitants in general ; so that even if the Mufti of Constantinople were to send a missionary to preach Mohammedanism to us, he would find a pulpit at his service.

Mr. Whitefield, in leaving us, went preaching all the way thro' the colonies to Georgia. The settlement of that province had lately been begun, but, instead of being made with hardy, industrious husbandmen, accustomed to labor, the only people fit for such an enterprise, it was with families of broken shop-keepers and other insolvent debtors, many of indolent and idle habits, taken out of the jails, who, being set down in the woods, unqualified for clearing land, and unable to endure the hardships of a new settlement, perished in numbers, leaving many helpless children unprovided for. The sight of their miserable situation inspir'd the

Benjamin Franklin

benevolent heart of Mr. Whitefield with the idea of building an Orphan House there, in which they might be supported and educated. Returning northward, he preach'd up this charity, and made large collections, for his eloquence had a wonderful power over the hearts and purses of his hearers, of which I myself was an instance.

I did not disapprove of the design, but, as Georgia was then destitute of materials and workmen, and it was proposed to send them from Philadelphia at a great expense, I thought it would have been better to have built the house here, and brought the children to it. This I advis'd ; but he was resolute in his first project, rejected my counsel, and I therefore refus'd to contribute. I happened soon after to attend one of his sermons, in the course of which I perceived he intended to finish with a collection, and I silently resolved he should get nothing from me. I had in my pocket a handful of copper money, three or four silver dollars, and five pistoles in gold. As he proceeded I began to soften, and concluded to give the coppers. Another stroke of his oratory made me asham'd of that, and determin'd me to give the silver ; and he finish'd so admirably, that I empty'd my pocket wholly into the collector's dish, gold and all. At this sermon there was also one of our club, who, being of my sentiments respecting the building in Georgia, and suspecting a collection might be intended, had, by precaution, emptied his pockets before he came from home. Towards the conclusion of the discourse, however, he felt a strong desire to give, and apply'd to a neighbour, who stood near him, to borrow some money for the purpose. The application was unfortunately [made] to perhaps the only man in the company who had the firmness not to be affected by the preacher. His answer was : "*At any other time, Friend Hopkinson, I would lend to thee freely ; but not now, for thee seems to be out of thy right senses.*"

Some of Mr. Whitefield's enemies affected to suppose that he would apply these collections to his own private emolument ; but I, who was intimately acquainted with him (being employed in printing his Sermons and Journals, etc.), never had the least suspicion of his integrity, but am to this day decidedly of opinion that he was in all his conduct a perfectly *honest man ;* and methinks my testimony in his favour ought to have the more weight, as we had no religious connection. He us'd, indeed, sometimes to pray for my conversion, but he never had the satisfaction of believing that his prayers were heard. Ours was a mere civil friendship, sincere on both sides, and lasted to his death.

The following instance will show something of the terms on which we stood. Upon one of his arrivals from England at Boston, he wrote to me that he should come soon to Philadelphia, but knew not where he could lodge when there, as he understood his old friend and host, Mr. Benezet, was removed to Germantown. My answer was : "You know my house ; if you can make shift with its scanty accommodations, you will be most heartily welcome." He reply'd, that if I made that kind offer for Christ's sake, I should not miss of a reward. And I returned : *" Don't let me be mistaken ; it was not for Christ's sake, but for your own sake."* One of our common acquaintance jocosely remark'd, that, knowing it to be the custom of the saints, when they received any favour, to shift the burden of the obligation from off their own shoulders, and place it in heaven, I had contriv'd to fix it on earth.

The last time I saw Mr. Whitefield was in London, when he consulted me about his Orphan House concern, and his purpose of appropriating it to the establishment of a college.

He had a loud and clear voice, and articulated his words and sentences so perfectly, that he might be heard and understood at a great distance, especially as his auditors, however numerous, observ'd the most exact silence. He preach'd one evening from the top of the Court-house steps, which are in the middle of Market-street, and on the west side of Second-street, which crosses it at right angles. Both streets were fill'd with his hearers to a considerable distance. Being among the hindmost in Market-street, I had the curiosity to learn how far he could be heard, by retiring back-

George Whitefield

wards down the street towards the river ; and
I found his voice distinct till I came near Front-
street, when some noise in that street obscur'd
it. Imagining then a semicircle, of which my
distance should be the radius, and that it were
fill'd with auditors, to each of whom I allow'd
two square feet, I computed that he might well
be heard by more than thirty thousand. This
reconcil'd me to the newspaper accounts of his
having preach'd to twenty-five thousand people
in the fields, and to the antient histories of generals haranguing whole armies, of which I had
sometimes doubted.

By hearing him often, I could distinguish
easily between sermons newly compos'd, and
those which he had often preach'd in the course
of his travels. His delivery of the latter was
so improv'd by frequent repetitions that every
accent, every emphasis, every modulation of
voice, was so perfectly well turn'd and well
plac'd, that, without being interested in the
subject, one could not help being pleas'd with
the discourse ; a pleasure of much the same
kind with that receiv'd from an excellent piece
of musick. This is an advantage itinerant
preachers have over those who are stationary,
as the latter cannot well improve their delivery
of a sermon by so many rehearsals.

His writing and printing from time to time
gave great advantage to his enemies ; un-
guarded expressions, and even erroneous opinions, delivered in preaching, might have been

afterwards explain'd or qualifi'd by supposing others that might have accompani'd them, or they might have been deny'd ; but *litera scripta manet.* Critics attack'd his writings violently, and with so much appearance of reason as to diminish the number of his votaries and prevent their encrease ; so that I am of opinion if he had never written anything, he would have left behind him a much more numerous and important sect, and his reputation might in that case have been still growing, even after his death, as there being nothing of his writing on which to found a censure and give him a lower character, his proselytes would be left at liberty to feign for him as great a variety of excellences as their enthusiastic admiration might wish him to have possessed.

The Franklin Stove.

In order of time, I should have mentioned before, that having, in 1742, invented an open stove for the better warming of rooms, and at the same time saving fuel, as the fresh air admitted was warmed in entering, I made a present of the model to Mr. Robert Grace, one of my early friends, who, having an iron-furnace, found the casting of the plates for these stoves a profitable thing, as they were growing in demand. To promote that demand, I wrote and published a pamphlet, entitled " *An Account of the new-invented Pennsylvania Fireplaces; wherein their Construction and Manner of Operation is particularly explained; their Advantages above every other Method of warming Rooms demonstrated; and all Objections that have been raised against the Use of them answered and obviated*," etc. This pamphlet had a good effect. Gov'r. Thomas was so pleas'd with the construction of this stove, as described in it, that he offered to give me a patent for the sole vending of them for a term of years; but I declin'd it from a principle which has ever weighed with me on such occasions, viz., *That, as we enjoy great advantages from the inventions of others, we should be glad of an opportunity to serve others by any invention of ours ; and this we should do freely and generously.*

An ironmonger in London, however, assuming a good deal of my pamphlet, and working it up into his own, and making some small changes in the machine, which rather hurt its operation, got a patent for it there, and made, as I was told, a little fortune by it. And this is not the only instance of patents taken out for my inventions by others, tho' not always with the same success, which I never contested, as having no desire of profiting by patents myself, and hating disputes. The use of these fire-places in very many houses, both of this and the neighboring colonies, has been, and is, a great saving of wood to the inhabitants.

Civic Pride.

Our city, tho' laid out with a beautifull regularity, the streets large, strait, and crossing each other at right angles, had the disgrace of suffering those streets to remain long unpav'd, and in wet weather the wheels of heavy carriages plough'd them into a quagmire, so that it was difficult to cross them; and in dry weather the dust was offensive. I had liv'd near what was call'd the Jersey Market, and saw with pain the inhabitants wading in mud while purchasing their provisions. A strip of ground down the middle of that market was at length pav'd with brick, so that, being once in the market, they had firm footing, but were often over shoes in dirt to get there. By talking and writing on the subject, I was at length instrumental in getting the street pav'd with stone between the market and the brick'd foot-pavement, that was on each side next the houses. This, for some time, gave an easy access to the market dry-shod; but, the rest of the street not being pav'd, whenever a carriage came out of the mud upon this pavement, it shook off and left its dirt upon it, and it was soon cover'd with mire, which was not remov'd, the city as yet having no scavengers.

Benjamin Franklin

After some inquiry, I found a poor, industrious man, who was willing to undertake keeping the pavement clean, by sweeping it twice a week, carring off the dirt from before all the neighbours' doors, for the sum of sixpence per month, to be paid by each house. I then wrote and printed a paper setting forth the advantages to the neighbourhood that might be obtain'd by this small expense ; the greater ease in keeping our houses clean, so much dirt not being brought in by people's feet ; the benefit to the shops by more custom, etc., etc., as buyers could more easily get at them ; and by not having, in windy weather, the dust blown in upon their goods, etc., etc. I sent one of these papers to each house, and in a day or two went round to see who would subscribe an agreement to pay these sixpences ; it was unanimously sign'd, and for a time well executed. All the inhabitants of the city were delighted with the cleanliness of the pavement that surrounded the market, it being a convenience to all, and this rais'd a general desire to have all the streets paved, and made the people more willing to submit to a tax for that purpose.

After some time I drew a bill for paving the city, and brought it into the Assembly. It was just before I went to England, in 1757, and did not pass till I was gone,* and then with an alteration in the mode of assessment, which I thought not for the better, but with an addi-

* See votes.—[Marg. note.]

tional provision for lighting as well as paving the streets, which was a great improvement. It was by a private person, the late Mr. John Clifton, his giving a sample of the utility of lamps, by placing one at his door, that the people were first impressed with the idea of enlighting all the city. The honour of this public benefit has also been ascrib'd to me, but it belongs truly to that gentleman. I did but follow his example, and have only some merit to claim respecting the form of our lamps, as differing from the globe lamps we were at first supply'd with from London. Those we found inconvenient in these respects : they admitted no air below ; the smoke, therefore, did not readily go out above, but circulated in the globe, lodg'd on its inside, and soon obstructed the light they were intended to afford ; giving, besides, the daily trouble of wiping them clean ; and an accidental stroke on one of them would demolish it, and render it totally useless. I therefore suggested the composing them of four flat panes, with a long funnel above to draw up the smoke, and crevices admitting air below, to facilitate the ascent of the smoke ; by this means they were kept clean, and did not grow dark in a few hours, as the London lamps do, but continu'd bright till morning, and an accidental stroke would generally break but a single pane, easily repair'd.

I have sometimes wonder'd that the Londoners did not, from the effect holes in the bottom of the globe lamps us'd at Vauxhall have in keeping them clean, learn to have such holes in their street lamps. But, these holes being made for another purpose, viz., to communicate flame more suddenly to the wick by a little flax hanging down thro' them, the other use, of letting in air, seems not to have been thought of ; and therefore, after the lamps have been lit a few hours, the streets of London are very poorly illuminated.

The mention of these improvements puts me in mind of one I propos'd, when in London, to Dr. Fothergill, who was among the best men I have known, and a great promoter of useful projects. I had observ'd that the streets, when dry, were never swept, and the light dust carried away ; but it was suffer'd to accumulate till wet weather reduc'd it to mud, and then, after lying some days so deep on the pavement that there was no crossing but in paths kept clean by poor people with brooms, it was with great labour rak'd together and thrown up into carts open above, the sides of which suffer'd some of the slush at every jolt on the pavement to shake out and fall, sometimes to the annoyance of foot-passengers. The reason given for not sweeping the dusty streets was, that the dust would fly into the windows of shops and houses.

An accidental occurrence had instructed me how much sweeping might be done in a little time. I found at my door in Craven-street, one morning, a poor woman sweeping my pavement with a birch broom ; she appeared very pale and feeble, as just come out of a fit of sickness. I ask'd who employ'd her to sweep there ; she said : " Nobody ; but I am very poor and in distress, and I sweeps before gentlefolkses doors, and hopes they will give me something." I bid her sweep the whole street clean, and I would give her a shilling ; this was at nine o'clock ; at 12 she came for the shilling. From the slowness I saw at first in her working, I could scarce believe that the work was done so soon, and sent my servant to examine it, who reported that the whole street was swept perfectly clean, and all the dust plac'd in the gutter, which was in the middle ; and the next rain wash'd it quite away, so that the pavement and even the kennel were perfectly clean.

I then judg'd that, if that feeble woman could sweep such a street in three hours, a strong, active man might have done it in half the time. And here let me remark the convenience of having but one gutter in such a narrow street, running down its middle, instead of two, one on each side, near the footway ; for where all the rain that falls on a street runs from the sides and meets in the middle, it forms there a current strong enough to wash away all the mud it meets with : but when divided into two channels, it is often too weak to cleanse either, and only makes the mud it finds more fluid, so that the wheels of carriages and feet of horses throw and dash it upon the foot-pavement, which is thereby rendered foul and slippery, and sometimes splash it upon those who are walking. My proposal, communicated to the good doctor, was as follows :

"For the more effectual cleaning and keeping clean the streets of London and Westminster, it is proposed that the several watchmen be contracted with to have the dust swept up in dry seasons, and the mud rak'd up at other times, each in the several streets and lanes of his round ; that they be furnish'd with brooms and other proper instruments for these purposes, to be kept at their respective stands, ready to furnish the poor people they may employ in the service.

"That in the dry summer months the dust be all swept up into heaps at proper distances, before the shops and windows of houses are usually opened, when the scavengers, with close-covered carts, shall also carry it all away.

"That the mud, when rak'd up, be not left in heaps to be spread abroad again by the wheels of carriages and trampling of horses, but that the scavengers be provided with bodies of carts, not plac'd high upon wheels, but low upon sliders, with lattice-bottoms, which, being cover'd with straw, will retain the mud thrown into them, and permit the water to drain from it, whereby it will become much lighter, water making the greatest part of its weight ; these bodies of carts to be plac'd at convenient distances, and the mud brought to them in wheelbarrows ; they remaining where plac'd till the mud is drain'd, and then horses brought to draw them away."

I have since had doubts of the practicability of the latter part of this proposal, on account of the narrowness of some streets, and the difficulty of placing the draining-sleds so as not to encumber too much the passage ; but I am still of opinion that the former, requiring the dust to be swept up and carry'd away before the shops are open, is very practicable in summer, when the days are long ; for, in walking thro' the Strand and Fleet-street one morning at seven o'clock, I observ'd there was not one shop open, tho' it had been daylight and the sun up above three hours ; the inhabitants of London chusing voluntarily to live much by candle-light, and sleep by sunshine, and yet often complain, a little absurdly, of the duty on candles, and the high price of tallow.

Some may think these trifling matters not worth minding or relating ; but when they consider that tho' dust blown into the eyes of a single person, or into a single shop on a windy day, is but of small importance, yet the great number of the instances in a populous city, and its frequent repetitions give it weight and consequence, perhaps they will not censure very severely those who bestow some attention to affairs of this seemingly low nature. Human felicity is produc'd not so much by great pieces of good fortune that seldom happen, as by little advantages that occur every day. Thus, if you teach a poor young man to shave himself, and keep his razor in order, you may contribute more to the happiness of his life than in giving him a thousand guineas. The money may be soon spent, the regret only remaining of having foolishly consumed it; but in the other case, he escapes the frequent vexation of waiting for barbers, and of their sometimes dirty fingers, offensive breaths, and dull razors; he shaves when most convenient to him, and enjoys daily the pleasure of its being done with a good instrument. With these sentiments I have hazarded the few preceding pages, hoping they may afford hints which some time or other may be useful to a city I love, having lived many years in it very happily, and perhaps to some of our towns in America.

Philosophical Experiments.

In 1746, being at Boston, I met there with a Dr. Spence, who was lately arrived from Scotland, and show'd me some electric experiments. They were imperfectly perform'd, as he was not very expert; but, being on a subject quite new to me, they equally surpris'd and pleased me. Soon after my return to Philadelphia, our library company receiv'd from Mr. P. Collinson, Fellow of the Royal Society of London, a present of a glass tube, with some account of the use of it in making such experiments. I eagerly seized the opportunity of repeating what I had seen at Boston; and, by much practice, acquir'd great readiness in performing those, also, which we had an account of from England, adding a number of new ones. I say much practice, for my house was continually full, for some time, with people who came to see these new wonders.

To divide a little this incumbrance among my friends, I caused a number of similar tubes to be blown at our glass-house, with which they furnish'd themselves, so that we had at length several performers. Among these, the principal was Mr. Kinnersley, an ingenious neighbor, who, being out of business, I encouraged to undertake showing the experiments for money, and drew up for him two lectures, in which the experiments were rang'd in such order, and accompanied with such explanations in such method, as that the foregoing should assist in comprehending the following. He procur'd an elegant apparatus for the purpose, in which all the little machines that I had roughly made for myself were nicely form'd by instrument-makers. His lectures were well attended, and gave great satisfaction ; and after some time he went thro' the colonies, exhibiting them in every capital town, and pick'd up some money. In the West India islands, indeed, it was with difficulty the experiments could be made, from the general moisture of the air.

Oblig'd as we were to Mr. Collinson for his present of the tube, etc., I thought it right he should be inform'd of our success in using it, and wrote him several letters containing accounts of our experiments. He got them read in the Royal Society, where they were not at first thought worth so much notice as to be printed in their Transactions. One paper, which I wrote for Mr. Kinnersley, on the sameness of lightning with electricity, I sent to Dr. Mitchel, an acquaintance of mine, and one of the members also of that society, who wrote me word that it had been read, but was laughed at by the connoisseurs. The papers, however, being shown to Dr. Fothergill, he thought them of too much value to be stifled, and advis'd the printing of them. Mr. Collinson then gave them to Cavé for publication in his *Gentleman's Magazine ;* but he chose to print them separately in a pamphlet, and Dr. Fothergill wrote the preface. Cavé, it seems, judged rightly for his profit, for by the additions that arrived afterward, they swell'd to a quarto volume, which has had five editions, and cost him nothing for copy-money.

It was, however, some time before those papers were much taken notice of in England. A copy of them happening to fall into the hands of the Count de Buffon, a philosopher deservedly of great reputation in France, and, indeed, all over Europe, he prevailed with M. Dalibard to translate them into French, and they were printed at Paris. The publication offended the Abbé Nollet, preceptor in Natural Philosophy to the royal family, and an able experimenter, who had form'd and publish'd a theory of electricity, which then had the general vogue. He could not at first believe that such a work came from America, and said it must have been fabricated by his enemies at Paris, to decry his system. Afterwards, having been assur'd that there really existed such a person as Franklin at Philadelphia, which he had doubted, he wrote and published a volume of Letters, chiefly address'd to me, defending his theory, and denying the verity of my experiments, and of the positions deduc'd from them.

Benjamin Franklin

I once purpos'd answering the abbé, and actually began the answer ; but, on consideration that my writings contain'd a description of experiments which any one might repeat and verify, and if not to be verifi'd, could not be defended ; or of observations offer'd as conjectures, and not delivered dogmatically, therefore not laying me under any obligation to defend them ; and reflecting that a dispute between two persons, writing in different languages, might be lengthened greatly by mistranslations, and thence misconceptions of one another's meaning, much of one of the abbé's letters being founded on an error in the translation, I concluded to let my papers shift for themselves, believing it was better to spend what time I could spare from public business in making new experiments, than in disputing about those already made. I therefore never answered M. Nollet, and the event gave me no cause to repent my silence ; for my friend M. le Roy, of the Royal Academy of Sciences, took up my cause and refuted him ; my book was translated into the Italian, German, and Latin languages ; and the doctrine it contain'd was by degrees universally adopted by the philosophers of Europe, in preference to that of the abbé ; so that he lived to see himself the last of his sect, except Monsieur B———, of Paris, his *élève* and immediate disciple.

What gave my book the more sudden and general celebrity, was the success of one of its

proposed experiments, made by Messrs. Dalibard and De Lor at Marly, for drawing lightning from the clouds. This engag'd the public
attention everywhere. M. de Lor, who had an
apparatus for experimental philosophy, and lec-
tur'd in that branch of science, undertook to repeat what he called the *Philadelphia Experiments ;* and, after they were performed before
the king and court, all the curious of Paris
flocked to see them. I will not swell this nar-
rative with an account of that capital experiment, nor of the infinite pleasure I receiv'd in
the success of a similar one I made soon after
with a kite at Philadelphia, as both are to be
found in the histories of electricity.

Dr. Wright, an English physician, when at
Paris, wrote to a friend, who was of the Royal
Society, an account of the high esteem my experiments were in among the learned abroad,
and of their wonder that my writings had been
so little noticed in England. The society, on
this, resum'd the consideration of the letters
that had been read to them ; and the celebrated
Dr. Watson drew up a summary account of
them, and of all I had afterwards sent to England on the subject, which he accompanied with
some praise of the writer. This summary was
then printed in their transactions ; and some
members of the society in London, particularly
the very ingenious Mr. Canton, having verified
the experiment of procuring lightning from the
clouds by a pointed rod, and acquainting them

with the success, they soon made me more than amends for the slight with which they had before treated me. Without my having made any application for that honor, they chose me a member, and voted that I should be excus'd the customary payments, which would have amounted to twenty-five guineas ; and ever since have given me their Transactions gratis. They also presented me with the gold medal of Sir Godfrey Copley for the year 1753, the delivery of which was accompanied by a very handsome speech of the president, Lord Macclesfield, wherein I was highly honoured.

Poor Richard's Almanac.

Poor Richard's Almanac.

["In 1732 I first published my Almanac, under the name of *Richard Saunders ;* it was continued by me about twenty-five years, commonly called *Poor Richard's Almanac.* I endeavored to make it both entertaining and useful ; and it accordingly came to be in such demand, that I reaped considerable profit from it, vending annually near ten thousand. And observing that it was generally read, scarce any neighborhood in the province being without it, I considered it as a proper vehicle for conveying instruction among the common people, who bought scarcely any other books ; I therefore filled all the little spaces that occurred between the remarkable days in the calendar with proverbial sentences, chiefly such as inculcated industry and frugality as the means of procuring wealth, and thereby securing virtue ; it being more difficult for a man in want to act always honestly, as, to use here one of those proverbs, *it is hard for an empty sack to stand upright.*

These proverbs, which contained the wisdom of many ages and nations, I assembled and formed into a connected discourse prefixed to the Almanac of 1757, as the harangue of a wise old man to the people attending an auction. The bringing all these scattered counsels thus into a focus enabled them to make greater impression. The piece, being universally approved, was copied in all the newspapers of the Continent ; reprinted in Britain on a broadside, to be stuck up in houses ; two translations were made of it in French, and great numbers bought by the clergy and gentry, to distribute gratis among their poor parishioners and tenants. In Pennsylvania, as it discouraged useless expense in foreign superfluities, some thought it had its share of influence in producing that growing plenty of money which was observable for several years after its publication."]

Franklin's Autobiography.

COURTEOUS READER.

I have heard that nothing gives an author so great pleasure as to find his works respectfully quoted by other learned authors. This pleasure I have seldom enjoyed. For though I have been, if I may say it without vanity, an *eminent* author of *Almanacs* annually, now a full quarter of a century, my brother authors in the same way, for what reason I know not, have ever been very sparing in their applauses ; and no other author has taken the least notice of me : so that did not my writings produce me some solid Pudding, the great deficiency of Praise would have quite discouraged me.

Poor Richard's Almanac

I concluded at length, that the people were the best judges of my merit ; for they buy my works : and besides, in my rambles, where I am not personally known, I have frequently heard one or other of my Adages repeated, with '' as *Poor* RICHARD says !'' at the end of it. This gave me some satisfaction, as it shewed, not only that my Instructions were regarded, but discovered likewise some respect for my Authority. And I own, that to encourage the practice of remembering and repeating those wise Sentences, I have sometimes *quoted my-self* with great gravity.

Judge, then, how much I must have been gratified by an incident I am going to relate to you !

I stopped my horse lately, where a great number of people were collected at a Vendue [*sale*] of Merchant's goods. The hour of sale not being come, they were conversing on the badness of the Times : and one of the company called to a clean old man, with white locks, '' Pray, Father ABRAHAM ! what do you think of the Times? Won't these heavy taxes quite ruin the country? How shall we be ever able to pay them? What would you advise us to?''

Father ABRAHAM stood up, and replied, '' If you would have my advice, I will give it you in short ; for *a word to the wise is enough,* and *many words won't fill a bushel,* as *Poor RICHARD* says.''

They all joined, desiring him to speak his

135

mind ; and gathering round him, he proceeded as follows :

Friends, says he, and neighbours ! The taxes are indeed very heavy ; and if those laid on by the Government were the only ones we had to pay, we might the more easily discharge them : but we have many others, and much more grievous to some of us. We are taxed twice as much by our IDLENESS, three times as much by our PRIDE, and four times as much by our FOLLY : and from these taxes, the Commissioners cannot ease, or deliver us by allowing an abatement. However let us hearken to good advice, and something may be done for us. *GOD helps them that help themselves,* as *Poor RICHARD* says in his *Almanac* of 1733.

It would be thought a hard Government that should tax its people One-tenth part of their TIME, to be employed in its service. But Idleness taxes many of us much more ; if we reckon all that is spent in absolute sloth, or doing of nothing ; with that which is spent in idle employments or amusements that amount to nothing. Sloth, by bringing on diseases, absolutely shortens life. *Sloth, like Rust, consumes faster than Labour wears ; while the used key is always bright*, as *Poor RICHARD* says. But *dost thou love Life ? Then do not squander time ! for that's the stuff Life is made of*, as *Poor RICHARD* says.

How much more than is necessary do we spend in sleep? forgetting that *the sleeping fox catches no poultry*; and that *there will be sleeping enough in the grave*, as *Poor RICHARD* says. If Time be of all things the most precious, *Wasting of Time must be* (as *Poor RICHARD* says) *the greatest prodigality;* since, as he elsewhere tells us, *Lost time is never found again*; and what we call *Time enough! always proves little enough.* Let us then up and be doing, and doing to the purpose : so, by diligence, shall we do more with less perplexity. *Sloth makes all things difficult, but Industry all things easy*, as *Poor RICHARD* says : and *He that riseth late, must trot all day; and shall scarce overtake his business at night.* While *Laziness travels so slowly, that Poverty soon overtakes him*, as we read in *Poor RICHARD* ; who adds, *Drive thy business! Let not that drive thee!* and

Early to bed, and early to rise,
Makes a man healthy, wealthy, and wise.

So what signifies *wishing* and *hoping* for better Times ! We may make these Times better, if we bestir ourselves ! *Industry need not wish!* as *Poor RICHARD* says ; and *He that lives on Hope, will die fasting. There are no gains without pains.* Then *Help hands! for I have no lands* ; or if I have, they are smartly taxed. And as *Poor RICHARD* likewise observes, *He that hath a Trade, hath an Estate*, and He that *hath a Calling, hath an Office of Profit and Honour* : but, then, the

Benjamin Franklin

Trade must be worked at, and the Calling well followed, or neither the Estate, nor the Office, will enable us to pay our taxes.

If we are industrious, we shall never starve, for, as Poor RICHARD says, *At the working man's house, Hunger looks in ; but dares not enter.* Nor will the Bailiff, or the Constable enter : for *Industry pays debts, while Despair increaseth them,* says Poor RICHARD.

What though you have found no treasure, nor has any rich relation left you a legacy, *Diligence is the Mother of Good-luck,* as Poor RICHARD says ; and *God gives all things to Industry.* Then

Plough deep, while sluggards sleep ;
And you shall have corn to sell and to keep,

says Poor DICK. Work while it is called to-day ; for you know not, how much you may be hindered to-morrow : which makes Poor RICHARD say, *One To-day is worth two To-morrows,* and farther, *Have you somewhat to do to-morrow ? do it to-day !*

If you were a servant, would you not be ashamed that a good master should catch you idle ? Are you then your own Master ? *Be ashamed to catch yourself idle !* as Poor DICK says. When there is so much to be done for yourself, your family, your country, and your gracious King ; be up by peep of day ! *Let not the sun look down, and say, " Inglorious, here he lies !"* Handle your tools, without mittens! Remember that *The cat in glove catches no mice !* as *Poor RICHARD* says.

'Tis true there is much to be done ; and perhaps you are weak handed ; but stick to it steadily ! and you will see great effects, For *Constant dropping wears away stones,* and *By diligence and patience, the mouse ate in two the cable,* and *little strokes fell great oaks* ; as *Poor RICHARD* says in his *Almanac,* the year I cannot, just now, remember.

Methinks, I hear some of you say, " Must a man afford himself no leisure ?"

I will tell thee, my friend ! what *Poor RICHARD* says.

Employ thy time well, if thou meanest to gain leisure ! and
Since thou art not sure of a minute, throw not away an hour !

Leisure is time for doing something useful. This leisure the diligent man will obtain ; but the lazy man never. So that, as *Poor RICHARD* says, *A life of leisure, and a life of laziness are two things.* Do you imagine that Sloth will afford you more comfort than Labour ? No ! for as *Poor RICHARD* says, *Trouble springs from idleness, and grievous toil from needless ease. Many without labour, would live by their Wits only ; but they'll break, for want of Stock* [*i.e.,* Capital]. Whereas Industry gives comfort, and plenty, and respect.

Benjamin Franklin

Fly Pleasures ! and they'll follow you ! The diligent spinner has a large shift, and

> *Now I have a sheep and a cow*
> *Everybody bids me " Good morrow."*

All which is well said by *Poor RICHARD.*

But with our Industry, we must likewise be Steady, Settled, and Careful : and oversee our own affairs *with our own eyes,* and not trust too much to others. For, as *Poor RICHARD* says,

> *I never saw an oft removed tree,*
> *Nor yet an oft removed family,*
> *That throve so well, as those that settled be.*

And again, *Three Removes are as bad as a Fire* ; and again *Keep thy shop ! and thy shop will keep thee !* and again, *If you would have your business done, go ! if not, send !* and again,

> *He that by the plough would thrive ;*
> *Himself must either hold or drive.*

And again, *The Eye of the master will do more work than both his Hands* ; and again, *Want of Care does us more damage than Want of Knowledge* ; and again, *Not to over-see workmen, is to leave them your purse open.*

Trusting too much to others' care, is the ruin of many. For, as the *Almanac* says, *In the affairs of this world, men are saved, not by faith, but by the want of it.* But a man's own care is profitable ; for, saith *Poor DICK, Learning is to the Studious,* and *Riches to the Careful* ; as well as *Power to the Bold,* and *Heaven to the Virtuous.* And further, *If you would have a faithful servant, and one that you like ; serve yourself !*

And again, he adviseth to circumspection and care, even in the smallest matters ; because sometimes, *A little neglect may breed great mischief :* adding, *For want of a nail, the shoe was lost ; for want of a shoe, the horse was lost ; and for want of a horse, the rider was lost* ; being overtaken, and slain by the enemy. All for want of care about a horse-shoe nail.

So much for Industry, my friends ! and attention to one's own business ; but to these we must add FRUGALITY, if we would make our industry more certainly successful. *A man may, if he knows not how to save as he gets, keep his nose, all his life, to the grindstone ; and die not worth a groat at last. A fat Kitchen makes a lean Will,* as *Poor RICHARD* says, and

Many estates are spent in the getting,
Since women, for Tea, forsook spinning and
  knitting ;
And men, for Punch, forsook hewing and
  splitting.

If you would be healthy, says he in another

Almanac, think of Saving, as well as of Getting! The Indies have not made Spain rich; because her Outgoes are greater than her Incomes.

Away, then, with your expensive follies! and you will not have so much cause to complain of hard Times, heavy taxes, and chargeable families. For, as *Poor DICK* says,

Women and Wine, Game and Deceit,
Make the Wealth small, and the Wants
    great.

And farther, *What maintains one vice, would bring up two children.*

You may think perhaps, that, a *little* tea, or a *little* punch, now and then; diet, a *little* more costly; clothes, a *little* finer; and a *little* entertainment, now and then; can be no great matter. But remember what *Poor RICHARD* says, *Many a Little makes a Mickle*; and farther, *Beware of little expenses! a small leak will sink a great ship*; and again, *Who dainties love; shall beggars prove!* and moreover, *Fools make feasts, and wise men eat them.*

Here are you all got together at this Vendue of Fineries and knicknacks! You call them Goods: but if you do not take care, they will prove Evils to some of you! You expect they will be sold cheap, and perhaps they may, for less than they cost; but if you have no occasion for them, they must be *dear* to you! Remem-

Poor Richard's Almanac

ber what *Poor RICHARD* says! *Buy what thou hast no need of, and, ere long, thou shalt sell thy necessaries!* And again, *At a great pennyworth, pause a while!* He means, that perhaps the cheapness is apparent only, and not real ; or the bargain, by straitening thee in thy business, may do thee more harm than good. For in another place, he says, *Many have been ruined by buying good pennyworths.*

Again, *Poor RICHARD* says, *'Tis foolish, to lay out money in a purchase of Repentance :* and yet this folly is practised every day at Vendues, for want of minding the *Almanac.*

Wise men, as *Poor DICK* says, *learn by others' harms ; Fools, scarcely by their own :* but *Felix quem faciunt aliena pericula cautum.* Many a one, for the sake of finery on the back, has gone with a hungry belly, and half starved their families. *Silks and satins, scarlet and velvets,* as *Poor RICHARD* says, *put out the kitchen fire!* These are not the necessaries of life ; they can scarcely be called the conveniences : and yet only because they look pretty, how many *want* to have them ! The artificial wants of mankind thus become more numerous than the natural ; and as *Poor DICK* says, *For one* poor *person, there are a hundred* indigent.

By these, and other extravagances, the genteel are reduced to poverty, and forced to borrow of those whom they formerly despised ;

but who, through Industry and Frugality, have maintained their standing. In which case, it appears plainly that *A ploughman on his legs is higher than a gentleman on his knees*, as *Poor RICHARD* says. Perhaps they have had a small estate left them, which they knew not the getting of. They think *'tis day ! and will never be night !* ; that *a little to be spent out of so much ! is not worth minding* (*A Child and a Fool*, as *Poor RICHARD* says, *imagine Twenty Shillings and Twenty Years can never be spent*) : but *always taking out of the meal tub, and never putting in, soon comes to the bottom.* Then, as *Poor DICK* says, *When the well's dry, they know the worth of water !* but this they might have known before, if they had taken his advice. *If you would know the value of money ; go, and try to borrow some !* For, *he that goes a borrowing, goes a sorrowing !* and indeed, so does he that lends to such people, *when he goes to get it in again !*

Poor DICK further advises, and says

Fond Pride of Dress is, sure, a very curse !
Ere Fancy you consult ; consult your purse !

And again, *Pride is as loud a beggar as Want, and a great deal more saucy !* When you have bought one fine thing, you must buy ten more, that your appearance may be all of a piece ; but *Poor DICK* says, *'Tis easier to suppress the First desire, than to satisfy All that follow it.* And 'tis as truly folly, for the poor to ape the rich, as for the frog to swell, in order to equal the ox.

> *Great Estates may venture more ;*
> *But little boats should keep near shore !*

'Tis, however, a folly soon punished ! for Pride that *dines on Vanity, sups on Contempt,* as *Poor RICHARD* says. And in another place, *Pride breakfasted with Plenty, dined with Poverty, and supped with Infamy.*

And, after all, of what use is this Pride of Appearance? for which so much is risked, so much is suffered ! It cannot promote health or ease pain ! It makes no increase of merit in the person ! It creates envy ! It hastens misfortune !

> *What is a butterfly ?   At best*
> *He's but a caterpillar drest !*
> *The gaudy fop's his picture just.*

as *Poor RICHARD* says.

But what madness must it be, to *run into debt* for these superfluities ?

We are offered, by the terms of this Vendue, Six Months' Credit ; and that, perhaps, has induced some of us to attend it, because we cannot spare the ready money, and hope now to be fine without it. But, ah, think what you do, when you run in debt ? *You give to another, power over your liberty !* If you cannot pay at the time, you will be ashamed to see your creditor ! You will be in fear, when you speak to him ! You will make poor pitiful sneaking excuses ! and, by degrees, come to lose your veracity, and sink into base downright lying ! For, as *Poor RICHARD* says, *The second vice is Lying, the first is Running into Debt :* and again, to the same purpose, *Lying rides upon Debt's back.* Whereas a free born Englishman ought not to be ashamed or afraid to see, or speak to any man living. But Poverty often deprives a man of all spirit and virtue. *'Tis hard for an Empty Bag to stand upright !* as *Poor RICHARD* truly says. What would you think of that Prince, or the Government, who should issue an Edict forbidding you to dress like a Gentleman or Gentlewoman, on pain of imprisonment or servitude? Would you not say that " You are free ! have a right to dress as you please ! and that such an Edict would be a breach of your privileges ! and such a Government, tyrannical !" And yet you are about to put yourself under that tyranny, when you run in debt for such dress ! Your creditor has authority, at his pleasure, to deprive you of your liberty, by confining you in gaol for life ! or to sell you for a servant, if you should not be able to pay him ! When you have got your bargain ; you may, perhaps, think little of pay- ment, but *Creditors* (*Poor RICHARD* tells us) *have better memories than Debtors* ; and, in another place, says, *Creditors are a super- stitious sect ! great observers of set days and times.* The day comes round, before you are aware ; and the demand is made, before you are prepared to satisfy it : or, if you bear your debt in mind, the term which, at first, seemed so long, will, as it lessens, appear extremely short. TIME will seem to have added wings to his heels, as well as shoulders. *Those have a short Lent,* saith *Poor RICHARD, who owe money to be paid at Easter.* Then since, as he says, *The Borrower is a slave to the Lender, and the Debtor to the Creditor* ; disdain the chain ! preserve your freedom ! and maintain your independency ! Be *industrious* and *free !* be *frugal* and *free !* At present, perhaps, you may think yourself in thriving circumstances ; and that you can bear a little extravagance without injury : but

For Age and Want, save while you may !
No morning sun lasts a whole day,

as *Poor RICHARD* says.

Gain may be temporary and uncertain ; but, ever while you live, Expense is constant and certain : and *'tis easier to build two chimneys than to keep one in fuel,* as *Poor RICHARD* says. So *rather go to bed supperless, than rise in debt !*

Get what you can ! and what you get, hold !
'Tis the Stone that will turn all your lead
    into gold !

as *Poor RICHARD* says. And when you have

got the Philosopher's Stone, sure, you will no longer complain of bad times, or the difficulty of paying taxes.

This doctrine, my friends! is Reason and Wisdom! But, after all, do not depend too much upon your own Industry, and Frugality, and Prudence ; though excellent things! For they may all be blasted without the Blessing of Heaven : and, therefore, ask that Blessing humbly! and be not uncharitable to those that at present seem to want it ; but comfort and help them! Remember, JOB suffered, and was afterwards prosperous.

And now to conclude. *Experience keeps a dear school; but Fools will learn in no other, and scarce in that!* for it is true, *We may give Advice, but we cannot give Conduct*, as *Poor RICHARD* says. However, remember this! *They that won't be counselled, can't be helped!* as *Poor RICHARD* says : and farther, that, *If you will not hear reason, she'll surely rap your knuckles!*

Thus the old gentleman ended his harangue. The people heard it, and approved the doctrine ; and immediately practised the contrary, just as if it had been a common sermon! For the Vendue opened, and they began to buy extravagantly ; notwithstanding all his cautions, and their own fear of taxes.

I found the good man had thoroughly studied

Poor Richard's Almanac

my *Almanacs*, and digested all I had dropped on those topics during the course of five and twenty years.   The frequent mention he made of me, must have tired any one else ; but my vanity was wonderfully delighted with it : though I was conscious that not a tenth part of the wisdom was my own, which he ascribed to me ; but rather the gleanings I had made of the Sense of all Ages and Nations.   However, I resolved to be the better for the Echo of it ; and though I had, at first, determined to buy stuff for a new coat, I went away resolved to wear my old one a little longer.   Reader ! if thou wilt do the same, thy profit will be as great as mine.

   I am, as ever,
    Thine, to serve thee !
     RICHARD SAUNDERS.
July 7, 1757.

Selected Essays.

Advice to a Young Tradesman.

To my Friend A. B.

As you have desired it of me, I write the following hints, which have been of service to me, and may, if observed, be so to you.

Remember that *time* is money. He that can earn ten shillings a day by his labour, and goes abroad or sits idle one half of that day, though he spends but sixpence during his diversion or idleness, ought not to reckon *that* the only expense ; he has really spent, or, rather, thrown away, five shillings besides.

Remember that *credit* is money. If a man lets his money lie in my hands after it is due, he gives me the interest, or so much as I can make of it during that time. This amounts to a considerable sum where a man has good and large credit, and makes good use of it.

Remember that money is of the prolific, generating nature. Money can beget money, and its offspring can beget more, and so on. Five shillings turned is six, turned again it is seven and threepence, and so on till it becomes a hundred pounds. The more there is of it, the more it produces every turning, so that the profits rise quicker and quicker. He that kills a breed-ing-sow, destroys all her offspring to the thousandth generation. He that murders a crown, destroys all that it might have produced, even scores of pounds.

Remember that six pounds a year is but a groat a day. For this little sum (which may be daily wasted either in time or expense unperceived) a man of credit may, on his own security, have the constant possession and use of a hundred pounds. So much in stock, briskly turned by an industrious man, produces great advantage.

Remember this saying, *The good paymaster is lord of another man's purse.* He that is known to pay punctually and exactly to the time he promises, may at any time, and on any occasion, raise all the money his friends can spare. This is sometimes of great use. After industry and frugality, nothing contributes more to the raising of a young man in the world than punctuality and justice in all his dealings ; therefore never keep borrowed money an hour beyond the time you promised, lest a disappointment shut up your friend's purse for ever.

The most trifling actions that affect a man's credit are to be regarded. The sound of your hammer at five in the morning or nine at night, heard by a creditor, makes him easy six months longer ; but if he sees you at a billiard-table, or hears your voice at a tavern when you should be at work, he sends for his money the next day ; demands it, before he can receive it, in a lump.

Advice to a Young Tradesman

It shows, besides, that you are mindful of what you owe ; it makes you appear a careful as well as an honest man, and that still increases your credit.

Beware of thinking all your own that you possess, and of living accordingly. It is a mistake that many people who have credit fall into. To prevent this, keep an exact account for some time both of your expenses and your income. If you take the pains at first to mention particulars, it will have this good effect : you will discover how wonderfully small, trifling expenses mount up to large sums, and will discern what might have been, and may, for the future, be saved, without occasioning any great inconvenience.

In short, the way to wealth, if you desire it, is as plain as the way to market. It depends chiefly on two words, *industry* and *frugality ;* that is, waste neither *time* nor *money*, but make the best use of both. Without industry and frugality nothing will do, and with them everything. He that gets all he can honestly, and saves all he gets (necessary expenses excepted), will certainly become *rich*, if that Being who governs the world, to whom all should look for a blessing on their honest endeavours, doth not, in his wise providence, otherwise determine.

An Old Tradesman.

The Whistle.

TO MADAME BRILLON.

Passy, November 10, 1779.

* * * * * I am charmed with your description of Paradise, and with your plan of living there ; and I approve much of your conclusion, that, in the mean time, we should draw all the good we can from this world. In my opinion, we might all draw more good from it than we do, and suffer less evil, if we would take care not to give too much for *whistles*. For to me it seems that most of the unhappy people we meet with are become so by neglect of that caution.

You ask what I mean ? You love stories, and will excuse my telling one of myself.

When I was a child of seven years old, my friends, on a holyday, filled my pocket with coppers. I went directly to a shop where they sold toys for children ; and, being charmed with the sound of a *whistle* that I met by the way in the hands of another boy, I voluntarily offered and gave all my money for one. I then came home and went whistling all over the house, much pleased with my *whistle*, but disturbing all the family. My brothers, and sis-

ters, and cousins, understanding the bargain I
had made, told me I had given four times as
much for it as it was worth ; put me in mind of
what good things I might have bought with the
rest of the money ; and laughed at me so much
for my folly, that I cried with vexation ; and
the reflection gave me more chagrin than the
whistle gave me pleasure.

This, however, was afterward of use to me,
the impression continuing on my mind ; so
that often, when I was tempted to buy some
unnecessary thing, I said to myself, *Don't give
too much for the whistle;* and I saved my
money.

As I grew up, came into the world, and observed the actions of men, I thought I met with
many, very many, who *gave too much for the
whistle.*

When I saw one too ambitious of court favour, sacrificing his time in attendance on
levees, his repose, his liberty, his virtue, and
perhaps his friends, to attain it, I have said to
myself, *This man gives too much for his
whistle.*

When I saw another fond of popularity, con-
stantly employing himself in political bustles,
neglecting his own affairs, and ruining them
by that neglect, *He pays, indeed,* said I, *too
much for his whistle.*

If I knew a miser, who gave up every kind of
comfortable living, all the pleasure of doing
good to others, all the esteem of his fellow-citi-

zens, and the joys of benevolent friendship, for the sake of accumulating wealth, *Poor man*, said I, *you pay too much for your whistle.*

When I met with a man of pleasure, sacrificing every laudable improvement of the mind or of his fortune to mere corporeal sensations, and ruining his health in their pursuit, *Mistaken man*, said I, *you are providing pain for yourself instead of pleasure ; you give too much for your whistle.*

If I see one fond of appearance, or fine clothes, fine houses, fine furniture, fine equipages, all above his fortune, for which he contracts debts and ends his days in prison, *Alas !* say I, *he has paid dear, very dear, for his whistle.*

When I see a beautiful, sweet-tempered girl married to an ill-natured brute of a husband, *What a pity*, say I, *that she should pay so much for a whistle !*

In short, I conceive that great part of the miseries of mankind are brought upon them by the false estimates they have made of the value of things, and by their *giving too much for their whistles.*

Yet I ought to have charity for these unhappy people, when I consider that, with all this wisdom of which I am boasting, there are certain things in the world so tempting, for example, the apples of King John, which, happily, are not to be bought ; for if they were put to sale by auction, I might very easily be led to ruin

The Whistle

myself in the purchase, and find that I had once more given too much for the *whistle*.

Adieu, my dear friend, and believe me ever yours very sincerely and with unalterable affection,

B. Franklin.

Necessary Hints to Those that Would be Rich.

Written Anno 1736.

The use of money is all the advantage there is in having money.

For six pounds a year you may have the use of one hundred pounds, provided you are a man of known prudence and honesty.

He that spends a groat a day idly, spends idly above six pounds a year, which is the price for the use of one hundred pounds.

He that wastes idly a groat's worth of his time per day, one day with another, wastes the privilege of using one hundred pounds each day.

He that idly loses five shillings' worth of time, loses five shillings, and might as prudently throw five shillings into the sea.

He that loses five shillings, not only loses that sum, but all the advantage that might be made by turning it in dealing, which, by the time that a young man becomes old, will amount to a considerable sum of money.

Again : he that sells upon credit, asks a price for what he sells equivalent to the principal and interest of his money for the time he is to be kept out of it ; therefore, he that buys upon credit pays interest for what he buys, and he that pays ready money might let that money out to use : so that he that possesses anything he bought, pays interest for the use of it.

Yet, in buying goods, it is best to pay ready money, because he that sells upon credit expects to lose five per cent by bad debts ; therefore he charges, on all he sells upon credit, an advance that shall make up that deficiency.

Those who pay for what they buy upon credit, pay their share of this advance.

He that pays ready money escapes, or may escape, that charge.

> A penny saved is twopence clear,
> A pin a day's a groat a year.

Motion for Prayers.

Dr. Franklin's motion for Prayers in the Convention assembled at Philadelphia, 1787, *to revise the then existing Articles of Confederation.*

MR. PRESIDENT,

The small progress we have made after four or five weeks' close attendance and continual reasonings with each other, our different sentiments on almost every question, several of the last producing as many *Noes* as *Ayes*, is, methinks, a melancholy proof of the imperfection of the human understanding. We indeed seem to *feel* our own want of political wisdom, since we have been running all about in search of it. We have gone back to ancient history for models of government, and examine the different forms of those republics which, having been originally formed with the seeds of their own dissolution, now no longer exist ; and we have viewed modern states all round Europe, but find none of their constitutions suitable to our circumstances.

In this situation of this Assembly, groping, as it were, in the dark, to find political truth, and scarce able to distinguish it when presented

to us, how has it happened, sir, that we have
not hitherto once thought of humbly applying
to the Father of Lights to illuminate our under-
standings? In the beginning of the contest
with Britain, when we were sensible of danger,
we had daily prayers in this room for the Divine
protection! Our prayers, sir, were heard; and
they were graciously answered. All of us who
were engaged in the struggle must have observed frequent instances of a superintending
Providence in our favour. To that kind Providence we owe this happy opportunity of con-
sulting in peace on the means of establishing
our future national felicity. And have we now
forgotten that powerful friend? or do we imagine we no longer need its assistance? I have
lived, sir, a long time; and the longer I live,
the more convincing proofs I see of this truth,
That GOD *governs in the affairs of men!*
And if a sparrow cannot fall to the ground without his notice, is it probable that an empire can
rise without his aid? We have been assured,
sir, in the Sacred Writings, that " except the
Lord build the house, they labour in vain that
build it." I firmly believe this; and I also believe, that without his concurring aid, we shall
succeed in this political building no better than
the building of Babel: we shall be divided by
our little partial local interests, our projects will
be confounded, and we ourselves shall become
a reproach and a byword down to future ages.
And, what is worse, mankind may hereafter,

Benjamin Franklin

from this unfortunate instance, despair of establishing government by human wisdom, and leave it to chance, war, and conquest.

I therefore beg leave to move,

That henceforth prayers, imploring the assistance of Heaven and its blessing on our deliberations, be held in this Assembly every morning before we proceed to business ; and that one or more of the clergy of this city be requested to officiate in that service.

[Note by Dr. Franklin.]—" *The Convention, except three or four persons, thought prayers unnecessary ! !*"

Letters.

To Dr. Priestley.

London, September 19, 1772.

DEAR SIR,

In the affair of so much importance to you,
wherein you ask my advice, I cannot, for want
of sufficient premises, counsel you *what* to determine ; but, if you please, I will tell you *how*.
When those difficult cases occur, they are difficult chiefly because, while we have them under
consideration, all the reasons, *pro* and *con*, are
not present to the mind at the same time ; but
sometimes one set present themselves, and at
other times another, the first being out of sight.
Hence the various purposes or inclinations that
alternately prevail, and the uncertainty that
perplexes us. To get over this, my way is, to
divide half a sheet of paper by a line into two
columns, writing over the one *pro* and over the
other *con :* then, during three or four days' consideration, I put down under the different heads
short hints of the different motives that at different times occur to me *for* or *against* the
measure. When I have thus got them all together in one view, I endeavour to estimate
their respective weights, and where I find two
(one on each side), that seem equal, I strike

Benjamin Franklin

them both out. If I find a reason *pro* equal to some *two* reasons *con* I strike out the *three*. If I judge some *two* reasons *con* equal to some *three* reasons *pro*, I strike out the *five ;* and, thus proceeding, I find at length where the *balance* lies ; and if, after a day or two of farther consideration, nothing new that is of importance occurs on either side, I come to a determination accordingly. And though the weight of reasons cannot be taken with the precision of algebraic quantities, yet, when each is thus considered separately and comparatively, and the whole lies before me, I think I can judge better, and am less liable to make a rash step ; and, in fact, I have found great advantage from this kind of equation, in what may be called *moral* or *prudential algebra.*

Wishing sincerely that you may determine for the best, I am ever, my dear friend, yours most affectionately,

B. FRANKLIN.

Mr. Strahan.

You are a member of Parliament, and one of that majority which has doomed my country to destruction. You have begun to burn our towns and murder our people. Look upon your hands ! they are stained with the blood of your relations ! You and I were long friends : you are now my enemy and—I am yours,

B. FRANKLIN.

To General Washington.

Passy, March 5, 1780.

SIR,

I received but lately the letter your excellency did me the honour of writing to me in recommendation of the Marquis de Lafayette. His modesty detained it long in his own hands. We became acquainted, however, from the time of his arrival at Paris ; and his zeal for the honour of our country, his activity in our affairs here, and his firm attachment to our cause and to you, impressed me with the same regard and esteem for him that your excellency's letter would have done had it been immediately delivered to me.

Should peace arrive after another campaign or two, and afford us a little leisure, I should be happy to see your excellency in Europe, and to accompany you, if my age and strength would permit, in visiting some of its most ancient and famous kingdoms. You would, on this side the sea, enjoy the great reputation you have acquired, pure and free from those little shades that the jealousy and envy of a man's countrymen and contemporaries are ever endeavouring to cast over living merit. Here you

To General Washington

would know and enjoy what posterity will say of Washington. For a thousand leagues have nearly the same effect with a thousand years. The feeble voice of those grovelling passions cannot extend so far either in time or distance. At present I enjoy that pleasure for you, as I frequently hear the old generals of this martial country (who study the maps of America, and mark upon them all your operations) speak with sincere approbation and great applause of your conduct, and join in giving you the character of one of the greatest captains of the age.

I must soon quit the scene, but you may live to see our country flourish, as it will amazingly and rapidly after the war is over. Like a field of young Indian corn, which long fair weather and sunshine had enfeebled and discoloured, and which in that weak state, by a thunder-gust of violent wind, hail, and rain, seemed to be threatened with absolute destruction ; yet the storm being past, it recovers fresh verdure, shoots up with double vigour, and delights the eye not of its owner only, but of every observing traveller.

The best wishes that can be formed for your health, honour, and happiness, ever attend you, from yours, &c.,

B. FRANKLIN.

To Dr. Mather, Boston.

Passy, May 12, 1784.

REV. SIR,

I received your kind letter with your excellent advice to the people of the United States, which I read with great pleasure, and hope it will be duly regarded. Such writings, though they may be lightly passed over by many readers, yet if they make a deep impression on one active mind in a hundred, the effects may be considerable. Permit me to mention one little instance, which, though it relates to myself, will not be quite uninteresting to you. When I was a boy I met with a book entitled *Essays to do Good*, which I think was written by your father. It had been so little regarded by a former possessor, that several leaves of it were torn out : but the remainder gave me such a turn of thinking as to have an influence on my conduct through life ; for I have always set a greater value on the character of a *doer of good*, than on any other kind of reputation ; and if I have been, as you seem to think, a useful citizen, the public owes the advantage of it to that book. You mention your being in your 78th year : I am in my 79th ; we are grown old

To Dr. Mather, Boston

together. It is now more than sixty years since I left Boston, but I remember well both your father and grandfather, having heard them both in the pulpit, and seen them in their houses. The last time I saw your father was in the beginning of 1724, when I visited him after my first trip to Pennsylvania. He received me in his library, and on my taking leave showed me a shorter way out of the house through a narrow passage, which crossed by a beam over head. We were still talking as I withdrew, he accompanying me behind, and I turning partly towards him, when he said hastily, *Stoop, stoop!* I did not understand him till I felt my head hit against the beam. He was a man that never missed any occasion of giving instruction, and upon this he said to me, *You are young, and have the world before you;* STOOP *as you go through it, and you will miss many hard thumps.* This advice, thus beat into my head, has frequently been of use to me ; and I often think of it when I see pride mortified, and misfortunes brought upon people by their carrying their heads too high.

I long much to see again my native place, and to lay my bones there. I left it in 1723 ; I visited it in 1733, 1743, 1753, and 1763. In 1773 I was in England ; in 1775 I had a sight of it, but could not enter, it being in possession of the enemy. I did hope to have been there in 1783, but could not obtain my dismission

Benjamin Franklin

from this employment here ; and now I fear I shall never have that happiness. My best wishes, however, attend my dear country. *Esto perpetua.* It is now blessed with an excellent constitution ; may it last for ever ! * * *

With great and sincere esteem, I have the honour to be, &c., B. FRANKLIN.

To the Bishop of St. Asaph's.

DEAR FRIEND,

I received lately your kind letter of November 27. My reception here was, as you have heard, very honourable indeed ; but I was betrayed by it, and by some remains of ambition, from which I had imagined myself free, to accept of the chair of government for the State of Pennsylvania, when the proper thing for me was repose and a private life. I hope, however, to be able to bear the fatigue for one year, and then retire.

I have much regretted our having so little opportunity for conversation when we last met.* You could have given me informations and counsels that I wanted, but we were scarce a minute together without being broken in upon. I am to thank you, however, for the pleasure I had, after our parting, in reading the new book† you gave me, which I think generally well written and likely to do good : though the reading time of most people is of late so taken up with newspapers and little periodical pamphlets, that

---

* At Southampton, previous to Dr. Franklin's embarking for the United States.
† Paley's Moral Philosophy.

few nowadays venture to attempt reading a quarto volume. I have admired to see that in the last century a folio, *Burton on Melancholy*, went through six editions in about forty years. We have, I believe, more readers now, but not of such large books.

You seem desirous of knowing what progress we make here in improving our governments. We are, I think, in the right road of improvement, for we are making experiments. I do not oppose all that seem wrong, for the multitude are more effectually set right by experience, than kept from going wrong by reasoning with them. And I think we are daily more and more enlightened ; so that I have no doubt of our obtaining, in a few years, as much public felicity as good government is capable of affording. * * * *

As to my domestic circumstances, of which you kindly desire to hear something, they are at present as happy as I could wish them. I am surrounded by my offspring, a dutiful and affectionate daughter in my house, with six grandchildren, the eldest of which you have seen, who is now at college in the next street, finishing the learned part of his education ; the others promising both for parts and good dispositions. What their conduct may be when they grow up and enter the important scenes of life, I shall not live to *see*, and I cannot *foresee*. I therefore enjoy among them the present hour, and leave the future to Providence.

To the Bishop of St. Asaph's

He that raises a large family does, indeed, while he lives to observe them, *stand*, as Watts says, *a broader mark for sorrow;* but then he stands a broader mark for pleasure too. When we launch our little fleet of barks into the ocean, bound to different ports, we hope for each a prosperous voyage; but contrary winds, hidden shoals, storms, and enemies, come in for a share in the disposition of events; and though these occasion a mixture of disappointment, yet, considering the risk where we can make no ensurance, we should think ourselves happy if some return with success. My son's son (Temple Franklin), whom you have also seen, having had a fine farm of 600 acres conveyed to him by his father when we were at Southampton, has dropped for the present his views of acting in the political line, and applies himself ardently to the study and practice of agriculture. This is much more agreeable to me, who esteem it the most useful, the most independent, and, therefore, the noblest of employments. His lands are on navigable water, communicating with the Delaware, and but about 16 miles from this city. He has associated to himself a very skilful English farmer, lately arrived here, who is to instruct him in the business and partakes for a term of the profits; so that there is a great apparent probability of their success. You will kindly expect a word or two about myself. My health and spirits continue, thanks to God, as when you saw me. The only complaint I then had does not grow worse, and is tolerable. I still have enjoyment in the company of my friends ; and, being easy in my circumstances, have many reasons to like living. But the course of nature must soon put a period to my present mode of existence. This I shall submit to with less regret, as having seen, during a long life, a good deal of this world, I feel a growing curiosity to be acquainted with some other ; and can cheerfully, with filial confidence, resign my spirit to the conduct of that great and good Parent of mankind who created it, and who has so graciously protected and prospered me from my birth to the present hour. Wherever I am, I always hope to retain the pleasing remembrance of your friendship ; being, with sincere and great esteem, my dear friend, yours most affectionately, B. FRANKLIN.

We all join in respects to Mrs. Shipley.